110651
F/BEL

The Pretender

for John and Pauline Lucas

The Pretender

David Belbin

Five Leaves Publications
www.fiveleaves.co.uk

The Pretender
by David Belbin

Published in 2008 by Five Leaves Publications,
PO Box 8786, Nottingham NG1 9AW
www.fiveleaves.co.uk

ISNB: 978 1 905512 51 5

Five Leaves acknowledges financial support
from Arts Council England

Five Leaves is a member of Inpress
(www.inpressbooks.co.uk),
representing independent publishers

Cover design: Darius Hinks
Typeset by Four Sheets Design and Print Ltd.
Printed in Great Britain

One

The first thing you need to hear about happened when I was fourteen. In English, we were reading *David Copperfield*. The rest of the class complained that it was too long. I joined in, but, secretly, I was enjoying myself, especially when Mr Moss told us about Victorian London, a place bursting with invention and energy yet, at the same time, squalid, even depraved. I had already decided that I would live in London one day.

We'd got to the end of chapter twelve when Mr Moss gave us a different kind of assignment.

'I'd like you,' he said, 'to pretend you *are* Dickens. Write the beginning of the next chapter. Read it first, if you like. Yours must be different. You have carte blanche to do what you like, plot-wise, but it must be in the style of Dickens.' Then he went on about Style for a while. I only half listened. Yes, I thought. I'd like to have a go at that.

In my bedroom, I scribbled away, losing track of time. When I'd written enough, I typed it up, using the Amstrad word processor my mother had bought for me, second hand, from an ad in the evening paper. As a computer, it was an embarrassment. You couldn't play games. I used it for typing out essays and writing fiction, though my efforts so far had been pitiful, deleted the next day. After two or three drafts, the Dickens imitation was done. I printed it off, pleased with myself, yet sure Mr Moss — one of those sarcastic, nit-picking teachers — would find plenty of flaws in my work.

A week later, when he was returning the assignment, Moss did something I'd never seen a teacher do before. He gave back everybody's homework but mine. Moss was a mild looking man, with a narrow nose, a small, wiry body and dark, greasy hair that he didn't have cut often enough. He returned to his desk, opened a drawer and lifted out my Dickens piece. The teacher raised it like a flustered referee holding up a red card.

'Trace,' he said, 'produced quite the most memorable piece of coursework that I have come across in my brief career as a teacher. So memorable, in fact, that I'd like to read it out to you.'

The other boys stared at me with contempt: smart arse Trace again, they were thinking. Then the teacher began to declaim my mock Dickens, using exactly the same tone and slightly exaggerated manner he used when reading bits of *David Copperfield* to us. I listened carefully, trying to pick up what I'd done wrong. Had I put in a modern word by mistake, or mixed up one of the character's names? Not that I could tell. When Moss stopped, I was half expecting to be congratulated.

'What did you think?' he asked the class.

There was the usual silence that greeted a question we hadn't already been told the answer to. This was a top set, but, even so, it didn't do to show off, or express an opinion that might be ridiculed by the teacher. So my classmates were silent.

'Didn't you find it convincing?' Moss asked, stressing each syllable in the final word in a way that might or might not be sarcastic. 'Don't you feel that Dickens would have been proud to write such prose at the tender age of — what is it now, Trace — fourteen?'

My youth regularly humiliated me. Some of the other boys in the class were already sixteen, but I had been put forward a year and my birthday wasn't until March. I stared furiously at the lid of my desk, oblivious to the teacher's footsteps. Mr Moss grabbed me from behind, yanked me up by the collar of my shirt and turned me to face the whole class.

'Wouldn't you say that the piece was too convincing?' he barked, choking me. 'All right, Trace, I want the truth. Where does it come from?'

'I made it up, Sir,' I pleaded.

'I made it up, Sir,' he repeated, mimicking my voice. 'You're a devious sod, Trace. You dug around until you found a description that might have fitted, changed a couple of names then copied it out. Do you take me for a fool, boy?'

'No, Sir.'

'Then tell me where it came from.'

'Honest, Sir, I made it up.'

Moss's small, beady eyes began to bulge. 'If that's your attitude, we'll see how you feel about it after a headteacher's detention.'

He got out one of the yellow forms and began to fill it in. When he got to the space marked reason for detention, he wrote one word: cheating.

'But I didn't cheat, Sir. I...'

I thought he was going to hit me. I was, perhaps because I had no father, terrified of male violence. On the rare occasions when I got into fights, I never hit back, only shielded myself from the worst blows. Now the teacher saw the fear in my eyes and took a deep breath.

'If you tell me where you took the piece from,' he told me, more temperately, 'I'll tear this up.'

I thought for a moment, desperately trying to recall the name of a Dickens book that wasn't in the school library.

'*The American Notes*', I muttered, shamefaced.

Moss smiled, vindicated. Then, as the bell rang, he took the yellow form and my coursework and methodically tore them into tiny pieces. These he let fall through his fingers into the bin, like a bird shitting. The class began to pack up, but, with a wave of his referee's arm, Moss halted them. He gave us a sermon about plagiarism in coursework, saying that, if we were caught cheating, even in such a seemingly minor manner as this, it would put all of our exam results at risk.

We were late out for lunch and the whole class blamed me.

Two

My mother and I lived in a terraced house at one end of a semicircle that bordered a small green. These houses were originally alms cottages for the poor. A housing association bought most of them as accommodation for the elderly. Kids at school used to tease me about living in an old folk's home. It was, I suppose, an odd place for a child to grow up. There were no other children, but I was doted on by the elderly residents. Mum, on the rare occasions she went out, had no shortage of baby-sitters.

She did have a shortage of boyfriends. My father was never spoken of. He had deserted Mum before I was born, giving her, I came to think, a deep distrust of men. Her own mother was a single parent. Gran died when I was five, so I barely remembered her. Mum was my entire family.

The house was full of books and Mum read to me every night until I was old enough to read fluently on my own. If I wanted more choice, I only had to go to the library where Mum worked. When I was young, she was strict about the times I could go to the library. It had to be once a week, when she was on duty. She said she didn't want me showing her up by behaving badly in her absence. But I wasn't a very naughty child.

Mum's library rule was like the trick she played with 'lights out'. By setting an early bedtime, Mum ensured that I sneaked a torch under the bedclothes so that I could keep reading. Fiction became a forbidden pleasure. By rationing library visits, Mum made me addicted to the places, so that, later in life, wherever I lived, the local library became my second home.

After the Dickens incident, it was a long time before I copied another writer's style. I read all the time, and couldn't help but write books in my head. I would tell myself the story of my imaginary life, the one where I got the girl and won the Nobel Prize for Literature, in the style of the author who I was reading at the time. Sometimes, in the night, I dreamt whole chapters of books, the words forming on the page as I read.

All that was a form of day dreaming. I started writing seriously in the Sixth form, after the school took us on a weekend visit to Paris. This was my first trip abroad. Paris in the spring was like stepping into a movie (we didn't have a TV at home, but Mum and I often went to the cinema). On returning, I immersed myself in French authors and American writers who had lived in Paris and began my own tentative jottings.

When university applications came up, I'd had enough of always being younger than everybody else on my course and deferred for a year. Mum wanted me to apply for Cambridge, but I refused. Cambridge would be full of rich, public school people. No matter how good I was, I'd always be an outsider, without the breeding, brilliance or money to fit it. I applied to London University instead, to study Eng Lit with French subsid. At the interview, I was asked why I wanted to be in London. Did I have friends there?

'No. I applied because I want to live here. I want to be a writer, and successful writers have to live in London.'

The interviewer asked who my favourite writers were. This was difficult. I didn't mention Dickens because he was too obvious. Ditto Shakespeare. Chandler and Collins were out because they wrote mystery fiction. Kurt Vonnegut was risky because he wrote sci-fi. So I brought up Hemingway, whose short stories I'd been reading on the train. Then I mentioned Joyce, because he was difficult (so far, I'd only read *Portrait of the Artist* and *Dubliners*).

'Playwrights?' he said.

'Beckett, of course.'

He raised an eyebrow and I thought that he was about to catch me out with a difficult question. I'd never seen a Beckett play, though I'd once tried to read *Waiting for Godot*. It was his prose I knew.

'Perhaps you ought to study in Paris rather than London,' the tutor said, his voice becoming kindly. 'Those three all made their names there.'

'Actually,' I replied, a decision forming only as the words spilled out of my mouth. 'That's where I intend to spend my year out.'

Three

Mum was reluctant to let me go. At the time, I thought she was being over protective, because I was only seventeen. Later I realised she knew something I didn't. I argued that I needed to become a fluent French speaker to do well at university. Mum knew this wasn't strictly true, but could see that I was itching to leave. In the end, she didn't put up a fight.

That summer, while waiting for my A level results, I worked in a warehouse packing clothes from a mail order catalogue. After seven weeks, I had enough money to set me up while I found a job in Paris. I passed my exams with top grades and deferred my university place. At the end of August, I filled a rucksack with clothes and books, promised to send regular postcards home, and bought an open return ticket to France.

Paris in September was unlike the place I'd visited the spring before. It seemed even bigger, more complicated and much more foreign. I wanted to think of myself as a resident and was disappointed to find large parts of the city entirely populated by tourists. Yet the place still impressed me more than London. There were the wide, grand streets, suitable for a capital city. The buildings were majestic, never merely ornate. Everything seemed to take place on an appropriate scale, whereas the London I knew was a cramped, crowded place. In time I would come to know and love its haunted, peculiar powers, but Paris was my first love.

I'd meant to take a room on the Left Bank. I wanted to live in the Seventh Arrondissement, as Hemingway and Fitzgerald had in the twenties, but the only places I found were asking as much for a night as I was prepared to spend for a week. I stayed in a Youth Hostel, sharing a dormitory with an endless array of strangers, snoring and farting and sometimes screaming in the night.

Getting a job wasn't like in the books, either. I'd read George Orwell's *Down and Out in Paris and London*. I was prepared, if necessary, to work as a dishwasher, as he had, but most places used machines. My French was good, but when I went to bars with jobs on offer, I was spoken to in a rapid fire barrage that I could barely follow. I came across no English workers I could go to for advice. Paris was awash with immigrants, mainly blacks from the country's former colonies. These were the people I was competing with for work. I found myself shocked by the casual cruelty with which they were treated.

After a week, I was on the verge of going home, but it was too soon to give up. I spent my savings visiting tourist spots, posted a second, resolutely cheerful postcard to my mother, and got over my shyness enough to say *je cherche du boulot* at any spot where I might find work. The American and British churches had notice boards advertising temporary jobs for expats. Those for teaching English as a foreign language required a qualification beyond my three A levels. Nevertheless I pushed myself into going along to a couple that didn't mention a TEFL certificate, only to be told I was too young even to be considered.

My confidence (and savings) ebbed by the day. I'd spent my whole life as the only male in the house. At the hostel, I was part of a herd, and didn't like it. The turnover was huge. After a week, I was a long term resident, yet remained as anonymous as when I'd arrived. The most depressing thing was that, after lights out at eleven, you couldn't read. I bought a torch and resorted to shining it under the bedclothes, as I had when a child. But most of my reading had to be done in parks or, when it was too cold, in the least expensive cafés I could find.

That was how I finally came upon a job. I was having an espresso in a quiet bar on Mo. St. Michel, reading Hemingway's posthumously published memoir of Paris, *A Movable Feast*, when a middle-aged American tourist sat down next to me.

'I'll bet you can tell me where to find Shakespeare and Co,.' he said.

I was about to make a joke about Stratford-upon-Avon when I realised he meant the bookshop, which used to be on the Left Bank and featured in the book I was reading. Its owner, Sylvia Beach, was the first to publish Joyce's *Ulysses*.

'I think it's closed down,' I told him, 'years ago.'

'No,' he told me, 'it's in my guide book. I just can't find the street.'

He handed me the book, and, sure enough, there was a listing for the shop, at 37 rue de la Bucherie, which, according to the pocket map I carried, was just round the corner. This version of Shakespeare and Co. had been open since the 1950s, the book said. I volunteered to help the American locate it and, after two false starts, we found a bustling place overlooking the Seine. There was an antiquarian store on the left and a store selling new books on the right. The latter was piled high with works in English. I pounced upon a paperback of Jeffrey Meyer's Hemingway biography and asked, as I was paying, whether there were any jobs going.

'Are you a writer?' the young Australian at the till asked. It was the first time anyone had put this question to me, so I answered it honestly.

'I'd like to be.'

'If you say you're a writer, and George likes you, he'll let you stay here. You have to help out and he expects you to read a book a day.'

'And all I have to do is pretend to be a writer?'

'If you want to be a writer, you wouldn't be pretending, would you?'

I didn't answer this. Lots of people thought they would be great writers if they could only be bothered to sit down and write. I'd written enough rubbish to know that writing wasn't easy. But I remained curious about the bookshop.

'How many people stay here?' I asked.

'At the moment? I think it's fourteen. There are less in the winter.'

'Where?'

'Everywhere. Look upstairs.'

After I'd paid for my book, I found the staircase hidden away at the back of the shop. A sign said that none of the books upstairs were for sale, but customers were welcome to use the library. The first floor was full of nooks and crannies. One was decorated entirely with letters and postcards from people who used to live in the shop. A room on the right had a table with two typewriters and, around a corner, a single bed. A youth my age was asleep on it. Every wall was piled high with bookshelves.

The room at the front was a formal, old fashioned library, with easy chairs, a table in the middle and a window over-looking the Seine. To the right was a door that had a substantial lock, but was ajar. I pushed it open. Across the stairwell, above the antiquarian store, was a room full of cardboard boxes. Standing over a table in the middle, looking through one of the boxes, was a grey-haired man in a checked shirt.

'Can I help you?' he asked, in an American accent. I knew at once that he was in charge. If he liked me, I could solve my work and accommodation problems in an instant. But I also knew that, much as I hated the hostel where I was staying, I was far too young and shy to cope with a dozen or more well travelled want-to-be-writers at close proximity. I was, for better or worse, a loner.

'I was looking for a job,' I said, 'but I gather the people who work here are all volunteers.'

The American laughed. 'Volunteers, that's one word for them. They're hiring at WH Smith's on Rue de Rivoli. You could try there.'

Next day I found myself working, thirty hours a week, at the Paris branch of Britain's biggest bookseller. My job was to unpack boxes. My co-workers and boss were French. They hardly spoke to me, so I wasn't improving my language skills and remained friendless, but I was used to being self sufficient. What mattered was I had a reason to stay in Paris.

The pay was only enough to live on if I found cheaper accommodation. A guy at work directed me to a dowdy house on the edge of Clichy, not far from the Sacre-Coeur. My room was on the top floor of a tall, off-white tenement in between an estate agent's and an artist's studio on Rue Joseph de Maitre, overlooking Montmartre cemetery. There was a cheap Indian restaurant at one end of the street and a taxi rank at the other, though I never once used a taxi. For transport I made the five minute walk to the Metro at the Place de Clichy, crossing the road bridge that bisected the cemetery. A good location, though the room itself wasn't much. I still had to share a tiny kitchen and bathroom, but I could read as late as I wanted and at last had an address to give my mother.

I worked six hour days five days a week, starting at ten and finishing at six, with an unpaid two hour break at lunch, when there were no deliveries. This became my time for mooching around the city, hoping to meet women or, at least, find inspiration. My new job gave me little opportunity for either. The only girls I met were shop assistants, and, as boyfriend material, I was beneath their consideration. They didn't ask a lot, but a full time job and a car were pretty much essential in any man, in France as much as in Britain.

There were many long, blank hours that could only partly be filled with letters home, reading and abortive attempts at writing fiction. Writing by hand wore me out. My handwriting was an ugly squiggle. Sometimes I had trouble reading it back to myself. I needed a computer, or, at least, a typewriter. It seemed to me then that, if your words looked good on the page, the rest would follow.

Most Sunday mornings, on a street two minutes walk from mine, there was a regular flea market. It took place in a covered market that, for the rest of the week, sold flowers and vegetables. Some of the stalls were taken by professional dealers. Others were run by people who had stuff they wanted rid of. It was there, some five weeks after my arrival, that I found the typewriter.

It was a portable Royal, an American model with a QWERTY keyboard rather than the French AZERTY.

'How old is it?' I asked the old woman behind the table.

'Seventy years old,' she told me, in French. 'I think it belonged to a lodger of my grandmother's. I found it in her attic when she died.' She shrugged. 'Not quite old enough to be an antique, they tell me, but something nice to put on your shelf, perhaps?'

I told her I was interested in using it. 'But I don't suppose you can still get the ribbons...'

'Oh yes, it's a standard size. And...' She pulled out an old cardboard box. 'I found this with the typewriter. Look.'

There were two spare ribbons, still wrapped in cellophane, and two packets of manuscript paper held together by ancient string.

'I'll throw these in with it. Two hundred francs.'

This was over twenty pounds — hardly a bargain, when most typewriters were being binned, rather than sold, but I had fallen for the machine. The ribbon stretched between the rollers was dried up and worn, but the other two should see me through the rest of my stay in Paris. I had taught myself to touch type on a computer keyboard. A typewriter shouldn't be too hard to use. I bargained her down to a hundred and fifty francs. Madame Devonier insisted on writing out a full receipt, for which I would later be very grateful.

A typewriter handles differently from a word processor. If you type too quickly the keys are liable to jam up, forcing you to get your fingers covered in ink while you untangle them. Writing requires physical effort. At first, I could only manage an hour before my fingers ached. The machine was also noisy. Other residents of the house complained if I typed after ten at night, or on Sunday afternoons when they were trying to sleep off lunch. I didn't blame them. Sometimes the typewriter's machine gun staccato gave me a headache.

The quality of my writing got no better. I began to wonder why I thought I could become a writer. Was it because, three years earlier, I'd imitated Dickens and fooled my English teacher? Before coming to France I'd found the Dickens file on my word processor and read the piece for the first time since Mr Moss tore it up. By now, I'd read much of Dickens. I could see how far my imitation fell short. My syntax was too simple. My similes were awkward. I had no grasp of historical detail. A kind of lucky fluency had fooled the teacher, but it didn't satisfy me.

I was still fascinated by Hemingway. Now I tried to write like him. He seemed an easier target than Dickens because of all the one and two syllable words he used, the repetitions. I soon realised that Hemingway could get away with repeating 'and' and 'but' only because they were part of a rhythm. There was a kind of poetry that was cumulative and easy to imitate, but hard to bring off successfully. Many had tried. Sometimes it seemed I could hear Hemingway's rhythms in every new American short story I read in *Granta* magazine. But the American authors at least made something of their own in the copying process. Not me.

I was given a week off for Christmas and went home, feeling like I'd learnt nothing in my three months away.

Four

At home, Mum fussed over me, saying how much older I looked and acted. She wanted me to say I'd really missed her. I did and I had, but you didn't say that sort of thing to your mother. Men always leave their mothers behind. There are fewer mothers than fathers in fiction and not very many of either. In real life, maybe, many men have their closest relationships with their mothers. But they don't write fiction about it.

Christmas passed. On the morning I was leaving, I found something sinister, tucked away at the back of the cupboard where I thought Mum might have put my sleeping bag. It was wrapped in a blanket, the way a baby might be protected by swaddling clothes. Beneath the blanket I found a fourteen inch, portable Sony TV set. I covered it up and never once mentioned the thing. Mum must get lonely, I told myself on the long journey back to Paris. The nights are long and the radio's not as good as it used to be. Still, I felt betrayed. I thought it was the first big secret she'd kept from me.

Back in Clichy, I had no idea why I'd returned. I was doing a job I could have been doing at home. I was missing New Year's Eve parties to spend the night in a cold room, alone. Everybody else in the house was out. I spent the last evening of the decade rereading *The Sun Also Rises* in conjunction with Carlos Baker's edition of Hemingway's letters and Meyer's biography of the writer, which I'd already devoured once.

There was one story about Hemingway in Paris that particularly fascinated me. What happened was this: in late 1922, Hemingway was living in Paris with his first wife, Hadley, who was several years his elder. Ernest was a journalist at the

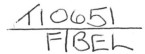

time and an aspiring, unpublished novelist who had already done much of the work that, when published, would make his early reputation.

Hemingway went skiing. Hadley travelled from Paris to Lausanne to join him. With her she brought a suitcase containing all of his manuscripts, including the carbon copies. Having secured a compartment on the train at the Gare de Lyon, Hemingway's wife went off to buy a London paper and a bottle of Evian. When she returned to the compartment, the suitcase was gone.

Hadley joined Hemingway in Lausanne. She was in a terrible state, and asked her husband to guess the worst thing that could possibly have happened. Hemingway thought for a moment that she had fallen in love with another man. But it was worse than that. The loss devastated Hemingway. He couldn't believe that Hadley had brought both the manuscripts and the copies, something she never explained. No-one knows exactly what was in the case. Hemingway once said there were eleven stories, a novel and some poems.

In *A Moveable Feast*, written just before he killed himself, Hemingway claims the loss was good for him. It forced him to start over and the fresh versions of the missing stories made his reputation. But it must have hurt terribly at the time and marked the first rupture of his relationship with Hadley.

As for my own writing, I didn't know if I was writing a comedy or a coming-of-age novel. How could I write such a thing? I hadn't come of age. As an experiment, I started to write my own versions of the missing stories. I thought that, by imitating Hemingway, I might learn something. I reread the stories from his first collection, *In Our Time*, and rewrote three from memory. Others I made up afresh, using details taken from my reading of the biography and later Hemingway.

In my notebooks, they weren't much. I threw endless pages away. Why should I think I was good at this? But when I began typing, the words that came out were my own, yet not my own. Carlos Baker, in his edition of the letters, listed Hemingway's most common grammatical, punctuation and spelling errors. I included a few of these, superstitiously thinking that, by making Hemingway's mistakes, some of his talent might rub off on me.

By February, I had written seven Hemingway stories and hated them all. Only two had any promise, I thought: an 'early' version of *Out of Season* and a 'new' story, untitled, where Nick Adams, Hemingway's hero from the *In Our Time* stories and many others, is in Paris. Like Hemingway, he is married, but his wife is away. Nick goes to meet another ex-pat who has been in the war. They spend an awkward evening together. I wrote it the way Hemingway used to write, with a pencil, then typed it out, trying to avoid any redundant words, to keep the sentences short and the tone authentic. Then I went back over it, cutting repetitions and phrases that seemed too modern. In the third sentence, 'could use' became 'was in need of'. Later, I changed the word 'chore' which sounded too English, into 'bind'.

I rewrote until I could no longer tell how well the piece read. Was the pace too jerky? I was pleased with the tone, but had no idea what to do with the plot, in which the Nick Adams character can't work out how to deal with his acquaintance, who is suffering the aftermath of shell shock. We'd studied First World War poetry at school, but I didn't know what it was like to be newly married, or fresh out of a war. Hemingway didn't write about his marriage in his early work. It was years before his fiction would broach the First World War. Nobody alive knew what he had tried, and failed, in those lost, early stories. Playfully, I inserted a grammatical error at the start of the second paragraph, where I had Hemingway write: 'there was a lot of people on the street'. This was a mistake I'd noticed Hemingway make in one of his best known stories, *Fifty Grand*.

I don't know why I aimed for such verisimilitude in my Hemingway pastiche. I'm not claiming that it was terribly good. I'd include a passage to demonstrate its mediocrity, but I'm unable to, for reasons that will appear in due course.

My New Year's resolution was to get another job. It didn't have to be a better one — I still had my university place lined up and was living pretty cheaply — but it had to be one where I met new people. If I couldn't teach, perhaps I could use my written French, at which I'd always excelled.

I went to a translation agency on Rue Saint-Lazare. The proprietor, a stylish, forty something brunette called Madame Blanc, told me I fell down on three scores: no degree, no computer, no experience. However, it was a very quiet day, so she offered me coffee. I pressed my luck and asked whether I could take the agency's translation test. Madame Blanc shrugged and said *bien sur*, then watched, amused, as I did it in ten minutes. She looked it over for thirty seconds before telling me I'd passed with flying colours.

'At least let me give you my address and phone number,' I said to Madame Blanc. 'Maybe something will come up.'

She could hardly refuse that. As I was writing it, Madame took a phone call. She spoke in English.

'No, we don't do that. I could give you a number, but most places are closed until next week. Wait, what exactly is it you want? Hold on.' She covered the receiver and spoke to me. 'Can you do French tuition? Teach somebody to speak French?'

'*Certainement.*'

It was the wrong way round, even I knew that. You want to learn French, you go to a Frenchman. But none of the people who'd taught me French at school were French. So why not?

'We have a young Englishman here,' she said. 'His French is very good. Would you like me to put him on?'

I found myself speaking to Paul Mercer.

'We're in.' there was a pause as he coughed and yelled for somebody called Helen. 'What's the name of this place? And your name is...? Well, Mark, would you be prepared to come to us for an interview?'

I asked Madame Blanc how much I should charge if I was successful and she suggested an hourly sum between four and five times as much as I was being paid at WHS. It seemed ridiculous but turned out to be more than reasonable.

'I'll owe you a commission,' I said.

'No need for that,' she said, flirtatiously, putting on an American accent, 'but you can come and see me sometime.'

Her smile made me blush. I assumed she was teasing me. It was years before I realised I was the kind of young man who attracted older women much more readily than those his own age.

Five

The Mercers were staying in an ancient hotel in St. Germain. Paul Mercer greeted me at the door of their spacious suite. He was fiftyish, wearing blue jeans and a plain T-shirt, with a full head of brown hair and warm, laughing eyes. To my mind, he dressed at least ten years younger than a man his age could get away with. His every sentence seemed to end with an exclamation mark.

'Mark! Why, you're so young! Come in, sit down, let me get you a drink!'

Paul poured on the charm. It would have been churlish to take a dislike to him. He was sipping brandy, though it wasn't yet midday, and added cognac to my coffee. Helen, he told me in his big, overfamiliar voice, was the daughter from his second marriage. He had just come out of his fifth.

'She can't stand her mother so I seem to have ended up with her, Helen!' he yelled at the bathroom door. 'Come and meet Mr Trace.' He turned back to me, draining his brandy in a single gulp. 'Done much of this kind of thing?'

Before I was forced to lie, Helen came into the room. From the way that Paul had been talking about her, I'd expected a sullen adolescent. Instead I found a beautiful gazelle, with long dark hair — I wasn't sure of the colour at first because her hair was wet. She wore only the towelling gown the hotel provided, which was noticeably too small for her. Helen looked me up and down. Her expression was disguised disdain at best, yet, smitten with her charms, I barely registered this. When Paul asked my rates, I quoted him the lowest end of the fee range suggested by Madame Blanc.

'Do you speak much French?' I asked Helen, who was brushing back her hair.

'Hardly,' she said. 'I'm an English Literature major.'

'I love literature,' I said, getting ready to warm to a theme. 'That's what I plan to study, in London.'

'Really?' she said, as though I were trying to catch her out, rather than chat her up. Within an hour, I discovered that Helen wasn't majoring in anything. She'd dropped out of two different universities. Paul said that he was trying to get her into the Sorbonne, but they wouldn't touch her unless she spoke fluent French. Which was where I came in.

All I had to do, Madame Blanc had assured me, was talk to Helen in French. But this wasn't going to be easy, for Helen had no French whatsoever. At my suggestion, while Helen dressed, Mr Mercer accompanied me to WH Smith, where I chose a French/English dictionary, a book on French Grammar and two copies of a textbook that looked similar to something I'd used in school aged thirteen. Mercer ('call me Paul') paid cash without looking at the books, being far more interested in eyeing up the female customers browsing in the store. Maybe he had come to Paris to find wife number six.

On our way back to the hotel, he asked if I was free for three hours every afternoon, five days a week. I did a quick calculation: I would earn twice as much as WH Smith paid me for half the work.

'It's a deal.'

When we got back to the hotel, Helen was dressed in jeans and a cashmere sweater. It had just gone two. Paul announced that he and I had come to an arrangement and I would be coming at this hour every day for three hours. He then paid me three days in advance and said that he had to go out.

'*Bon chance*,' he added, at the door, leaving Helen and me alone.

'Three hours is a long time,' she said.

I agreed. 'We can allow ourselves a break in the middle.'

'Paul won't know what we've been up to anyway. Teach me to say something.'

We went through *hello, how are you* and *what's your name.* Soon we were calling each other *tu.* Then we went on to age. When Helen asked me *quelle age as-tu?* I decided to go with the oldest age I thought I could get away with, and told her I was nineteen. Then I asked her her age. She told me she was twenty. I claimed that I turned twenty in March (I would actually be eighteen) and she seemed to believe me. We were more or less the same age — and we were to be in each other's company five days a week. What better chance would I get?

Our conversation soon faltered. At school, I realised, I had paid no attention to teaching methods. French relied largely on responding to tapes in language laboratories. I had no cassettes, and could see that Helen wouldn't have the patience to use them. Not that Helen wouldn't talk. Once Helen had decided she liked me, it was hard to get a word in edgeways. It was only when I mentioned the Sorbonne, that Helen got irritated.

'I'm not really going to get into the Sorbonne. That's Paul's excuse to have me here while he spends the afternoons drinking, doing deals with his buddies.'

'What does Paul do?'

'He's an... Art dealer, I guess you'd call it.'

Next day, with the advance Paul had given me, I bought a new shirt and wore it to the Mercers' hotel suite. It was two in the afternoon but Helen still gave the impression of having only just got up. She ordered a large pot of coffee from room service, occupying the time before it arrived by brushing her luxuriant hair. I watched the back of her head, tongue-tied. The coffee, when it came, was so lethally strong, I couldn't get through a cup. While she tied back her hair, I began talking in simple French. Helen drank cup after cup of the strong coffee. With each gulp, she seemed to thaw, responding to my questions in monosyllables at first, then muttered phrases. After a while, I managed to drag whole sentences out of her. As the coffee kicked in, her eyes lit and she talked in paragraphs, then pages — though, unfortunately, few of them were in French. She told me about bands she'd seen, drugs she'd taken, even boys she'd slept with, making me feel terribly *naïf*.

I can still picture Helen during those early afternoons together. She was waspish one minute, gossipy and flirtatious the next. In the hotel room, after that first meeting when she'd come from the shower, she always dressed simply and kept her hair tied back, making her profile more angular. She had high cheekbones, but her nose was roman and her brown eyes were a little too close together, a detail that stopped her from being a classic beauty. Yet this fault only made me the more obsessed with her. I decided I could only love flawed things.

Weeks passed. I made little headway as a potential boyfriend. When I enquired of Helen what she did in the evenings, she was vague to the point of becoming irritating. I don't want to give the impression that she was stupid. The opposite. Helen picked up French quickly and had opinions about most things she'd read, heard or seen. I lent her books and we'd talk about them. I couldn't converse with her about TV shows, but she was keen on movies, so, after a fortnight, I suggested that we go to one together. 'It's a good way to pick up more French,' I added. 'All the Hollywood films are dubbed into French.'

Helen thought this was a good idea. However, instead of going in the evenings, as I suggested, she insisted that we go during our lesson times. 'Paul will be fine with it. Don't worry'. I never checked whether Paul was 'fine with it', as I only saw him on Mondays now. This was when he paid me, a week in advance. Helen gave the impression she could wrap her father around her little finger, so we started going to matinees: first once, then twice a week.

In the cinema, our legs didn't brush close together. We didn't hold hands. Even in scary or suspense filled scenes, there was no physical contact. Helen was unshockable. Sometimes, though, she would hook her arm through mine as we walked back to the hotel.

'I try to get Paul to go to the movies,' she told me, as we left the engrossing *Monsieur Hire*, one of the few French movies I persuaded her to see, 'but he says his French isn't up to it. I tell him, it's all about the images anyway. I mean, he takes me to the opera, though neither of us speaks a word of Italian.'

'Maybe I should teach him too,' I said.

'Yeah, like he'd allow anyone to teach him anything. Listen, you want to go see the Rolling Stones? Paul was going to take me but he's got some thing in Milan. I don't want to go on my own. It's at the Parc des Princes.'

I'd seen the posters and knew the date.

'It's on my birthday,' I told her.

'Oh, then I guess you have plans.'

'No, I'd love to.'

Six

While I had a crush on Helen, a fourteen year old called Francine had a crush on me. I'd picked up some more tuition work from my connection with Mme Blanc. I spent an hour two lunchtimes a week with her friend, Philippe, a travel agent. We met in a cafe not far from Helen's hotel, so I could go straight from one job to another. It was Philippe who put me on to Francine's parents, both of whom had jobs in the government. Their daughter needed to catch up on her English because she'd lost six months of school after a scare with meningitis. 'She's a pretty girl,' Philippe warned me, 'An only child, so they're overprotective. But don't worry, I've told the father you're homosexual.'

I blushed and he added, 'you are, aren't you?'

I shook my head. Was this why I had so little luck with girls? Did they see my long hair, my fresh, innocent face, and, like Philippe, assume that I was gay?

'Don't tell them that,' Philippe warned, 'or you'll lose the job.'

I went to Francine's every Tuesday and Thursday evening, from seven to nine. Having three jobs meant I was now earning enough money to put some aside for university. Francine was pretty, in a tomboyish way. She was tall and thin, with long brown hair. Faint freckles and the last remnants of puppy fat were fast disappearing from her face. She wasn't what I thought of as my type, even if I hadn't already been hung up on Helen. I went for women who were mysterious and Francine was frighteningly straightforward. But she had admirers. Boys often showed up when I was round there, though they were never allowed through the door. Before long, I was sure, they would be knocking it down.

Francine was shy at first. Working with her was less fulfilling than working with Helen, whose French improved in leaps and bounds, making our conversations more of a challenge for me. At first, Francine's English was hard to stretch beyond simple grammar and phrases she'd picked up from TV and films.

Initially Francine's parents would be in the next room, looking in now and then. As the weeks went by, however, their busy social and professional lives meant that they often went out shortly after my arrival. When we were alone in the house, Francine became giggly and — as her English improved — flirtatious. Her main interests were getting me to do her homework for her and 'curing' me of my homosexuality, which her parents had told her about. She would 'accidentally' brush against me or lean over me to look at a passage, making sure that her small breasts pressed against my upper arm. As a teacher, I should have stopped her, but I didn't know how to. Anyway, I enjoyed it.

Philippe told me that Francine had a crush on me.

'Her parents have noticed and they are worried. I had to — assure? reassure? — them that you are not *bisexuel*. You haven't done anything with her, have you?'

'Certainly not.'

But I could have, if I'd wanted to. Francine became more worldly by the week. She asked about my other students. When I mentioned Philippe, she told me he was having an affair with her mother.

'I've heard Mum and Dad arguing about him.'

'I thought the French were meant to be liberal about that kind of thing?'

'That's a — what was the word you taught me? Stereotype. My mother is relaxed about sex, but my father's parents were Jesuits. He wants me to stay a virgin until I am married.'

31

She burst into hysterical laughter, which I didn't join in. The way my love life was going, she would lose her virginity before I did.

When I had to cancel a lesson because of the Stones concert, Francine threw a playful fit.

'Why can't you take me? Who are you going with?'

'The friend who gave me the ticket.'

'*Un ami ou une amie?*'

'What does it matter?'

'Because if it's *une amie*, I'll kill her!'

I changed the subject, before the game we were playing got out of hand.

On our way to the concert I told Helen about Francine and asked for her advice. I was hoping another girl's interest in me might make spark some jealousy in Helen.

'Is she attractive?' Helen asked.

'Very.'

'Physically mature?'

'Yes.'

'Then have an affair with her.'

'She's not fifteen yet. It's against the law.'

The age of consent was fifteen in France, but such details didn't bother Helen. She sighed with exasperation. 'Lots of things are against the law. It makes doing them more interesting.'

Our seats for the concert were poor. Helen said it was like watching a video on a TV set placed two hundred yards away in an open field. Half an hour in, she suggested we leave.

'Where do you want to eat?' she asked.

'I don't mind.'

'I can cook, you know. That's one of the things I miss about living in a hotel. Have you got a kitchen?'

'I share one, yes. But I don't have much food in.'

'There are supermarkets that open late.'

Having Helen cook for me wasn't an appealing prospect. I'd been looking forward to a candlelit, romantic meal. Yet, if I got her back to my room, possibilities might present themselves.

'My place isn't up to much,' I told her.

'I should hope not, or we'd be paying you too well.'

We took the Metro to Clichy and found a small branch of Champion that opened late. Helen bought mushrooms and button onions, rice, steak, a red pepper, garlic, a can of tomatoes, soured cream, three kinds of cheese and two bottles of red wine.

We ambled back to my room, with Helen talking about Henry Miller and Anaïs Nin and me talking about Hemingway. She was halfway through the Meyer biography I'd pressed on her.

'This isn't so bad,' she said, as I turned on the timed light on the ground floor.

'It gets worse.'

I ushered Helen straight into the cramped, grimy kitchen and told her I was going to put the heating on in my room. There, I removed the three eighteenth birthday cards I'd got from home, made the bed, and quickly cleared my small table so we could eat on it. I was putting the gas fire on when Helen wandered in, holding both bottles of wine.

'This is cosy,' she said. 'But only a single bed. Poor you. I was looking for some plain flour. Do you have any?'

I shook my head. 'I'm sorry the kitchen's so basic.'

'I'll manage somehow,' Helen told me, handing over the wine. 'Open one of these and put them both by the fire. You can't drink red wine cold.'

I managed to find a packet of flour in somebody else's cupboard, then helped Helen to chop vegetables. The kitchen was chilly, so she kept her leather jacket on. When she splattered herself opening a can, I had to dab tomato juice off it. This was the closest we came to touching.

'Cooking always makes me ravenous,' she said. 'Let's have some cheese.'

While we cooked, we ate hard cheese and drank cold wine, some of which went into the pot. After twenty minutes or so, we'd finished preparing the stew. Helen said it would take at least an hour to cook. The cheese and wine had taken me past hunger, into drunken arousal. Maybe it had had the same effect on Helen. I would never have a better chance than this. Helen followed me into my room.

'You weren't kidding,' Helen said. 'No TV.'

She fiddled with the radio until she found a jazz station she liked. Then she noticed something. Some sheets of paper had fallen onto the floor when I moved the typewriter from the table.

'What's this?'

She picked them up and looked at the papers before I could think of an excuse to stop her.

'It's Hemingway, isn't it?'

They were pages from the stories I'd forged earlier in the year. I said nothing. Looking at her looking at them, I felt my credibility sink. I had mentioned to Helen that I planned to be a writer. But this was the work of a copyist. I tried to find the words for an explanation. What was the point? I could see how absurd it would sound — I was copying Hemingway from memory to improve my style.

'Where did you get these?' Helen asked.

'I found them,' I lied. The typewriter was tucked away under my bed, so this story might stand up.

'Where?' She was alert with interest now, flicking through the pages. 'I recognise this first one. It's in an anthology we had to do at school. Where's the other from?'

34

'I don't know,' I mumbled, for the 'other' was all my own work, the story I'd given up. The words were bound to be trite, an obvious pastiche.

'It's probably not by Hemingway,' I added. 'It isn't in any of the collections I've come across.'

Helen was reading intently. 'It's obviously Hemingway,' she said. 'The style sticks out a mile. Where did you say you found these?'

'I didn't. A flea market. They were tucked inside some old magazines.'

This story was feeble, but it was the best I could come up with at such short notice. Helen seemed satisfied.

"That explains why the paper feels old, but the print looks quite fresh. You know what these are, don't you? It's in that biography you lent me.'

Helen told me the story of Hadley leaving the briefcase on the train.

'Do you know how important these could be? We've got to find the rest. Where was the flea market? What magazines were they in?'

I tried to obfuscate but Helen always got what she wanted. Soon we had arranged to meet on Sunday, when we would go the flea market and look for 1950's issues of *Paris Match*. Helen poured more wine.

'Can I take these home with me to read properly?'
'Sure.'

I found her an A4 envelope. Helen carefully put the pages into it, then inserted the envelope into a thick magazine so that the stories wouldn't get creased. She drained her glass.

'Now you'd better walk me to the Metro.'

'But we haven't eaten. The trains run for another hour yet.'

'I'm excited,' Helen said, drunkenly. 'I've lost my appetite. Anyway, old Paul will be angry if he gets back and I'm not home. We don't want him thinking that you and me have been up to any hanky-panky, do we?'

This was the first time that she'd allowed the possibility of our being romantically connected.

'Why not?' I said, 'Now that we're the same age?'

She gave me a look that was sad yet somehow scornful. Did she knew how much I wanted her?

'I'll be twenty-one soon,' was all she said.

It was the same thing as at school. Girls always wanted someone older than them.

I walked Helen to the Metro and waited with her for the train to come in. As it pulled to a halt, she kissed me on the forehead. 'Enjoy your ragout, birthday boy.'

Then she left with my stories.

The flame on the stove couldn't be turned down really low, so the stew had nearly boiled dry by the time I got back. I stirred in the last of the wine and ate a bowlful with a hunk of bread. Helen, it turned out, was a good cook. Still, I couldn't finish my meal, which was far too rich for me.

Next day, when I arrived at the hotel, at two the next day, Paul was in the suite, with Carlos Baker's Hemingway biography open in front of him. Helen was nowhere in sight. Before speaking, Paul looked me up and down, as if sizing me up for a new set of clothes. His voice took on a warm, fraternal tone.

'I'd like you to tell me more about how you found these stories, son.'

Seven

I don't know how convinced Paul was by my cock and bull story about the stories falling out from old copies of *Paris Match*. Nevertheless, he said he'd accompany Helen and I to the flea market on Sunday morning.

'Why?' I asked. 'Are you a big Hemingway fan, too?'

He gave me a puzzled but undoubtedly suspicious look.

'Mark,' he said, 'Have you any idea how much those manuscripts might be worth?'

'No.' I couldn't see how a few typewritten sheets could have any monetary value.

'I've rung the States, checking out those short stories. That second, untitled one, it was never published.'

'Maybe he changed the title.'

'I don't think so. I think he forgot about it, never rewrote it. If the manuscript's genuine, an awful lot of people will be interested in reading that story.'

'Genuine? Who'd forge a Hemingway story and hide it in an old magazine?' I asked, looking for a hint of suspicion on his face, but seeing none.

'Makes no sense to me, son. That's why I want to go and see if we can find some more. Maybe if we find the seller, we'll get an explanation.'

I nodded, preoccupied with how to handle the situation on Sunday.

'I hope you don't mind,' Paul went on, 'but I've passed the stories on to a man I know who can do certain tests on them — age of paper, all that kind of thing.'

That was it then. The paper and the typewriter might be old enough, but the pages were freshly typed. That was bound to show. By Sunday, Paul would know that I'd faked them.

Should I tell him now?

Maybe I would have done had it not been that, just then, Helen walked in. For the first time during an afternoon, her hair was down. She wore a long dress and looked ravishing. 'I thought we might go to a movie,' she said.

Paul smiled his assent. 'You kids have fun. Oh, and Mark, I gather that it was your birthday yesterday. You're not a teenager any more.'

'That's right.'

'Congratulations. Here, I want you to have this.'

He handed me a small, oblong box, which I opened. Inside was a gold plated, Swiss watch, a hundred times better than the scratched Timex I was wearing.

'Turn it over,' Helen said.

Engraved on the back in were the words: *Happy 20th, Mark, from H & P.*

'That's wonderful,' I said, wondering how I would ever explain the inscription to my mother. Paul grinned. Helen kissed me on the cheek. Last night the forehead, today the cheek — at least she was getting closer to the lips.

The two of us went to see a blockbuster on Boulevard Montparnasse. I think it must have been dubbed into French but there was so little dialogue, I hardly noticed what language it was in. As I walked Helen back to the hotel, I had the sensation that we were being followed. I meant to look back, but just then Helen put her arm through mine. I wished I had the courage to slip my arm around her waist, but I didn't.

Next day, Paul telephoned to say that he and Helen had been called away. Helen would have to miss two lessons, but they would be back to meet me on Sunday, as planned.

Eight

'Nice watch,' Francine said, in English, when I went to deliver her lesson that night. 'Did your rich boyfriend give it to you?'

'I don't have a boyfriend,' I told her.

'Poor you. Take it off. Let me have a proper look.'

She reached over and grabbed my wrist just as her mother opened the door to say that she was on her way out. Mme Gabin gave me a funny look.

'Look at Mark's watch!' Francine said, and Mme Gabin smiled, because she was using English. I told her it was a birthday present.

'You had a birthday? Your eighteenth?'

The agency had told the Gabins my real age.

'Yes.'

'Then we should give you a pay rise. I'll discuss it with my husband. Congratulations, Mark. Francine, *cherie*, we'll be back very late.'

'We should have a drink to celebrate,' Francine said, when they'd gone.

'My birthday was two days ago.'

'So what?'

'You're too young to drink,' I said, then felt stupid, because Francine had probably been drinking wine since she was a child.

Francine left the room without speaking. I started looking at the homework she'd done for me, correcting it closely. I found where she was up to in her English textbook from school. Her marks were improving. I hardly noticed that ten minutes had passed since Francine had gone out. Then she came back in.

Francine had brushed her hair and put on make-up. Her jeans had been replaced by a short black skirt with a tight dark blouse to match. I had never seen her like this before — fourteen going on twenty-five. In her hands were a bottle of champagne and two flute glasses.

'Do you know how to open it?' she asked.

'Your parents will miss the bottle,' I said.

'They have plenty. I've already replaced the one in the fridge. They wouldn't care... I mean, mind... anyway. We have champagne on special occasions. An eighteenth birthday is a special occasion, is it not?'

'I guess it is.'

Francine was right. I ought to celebrate. Tuesday night had been a wash-out. Helen had been more interested in the Hemingway manuscript than she was in me. But I wasn't as naive as she and her 'Art dealer' father thought. The watch was a bribe, not a present. They wanted me to lead them to the rest of the Hemingway stories. They'd sell them and keep most of the proceeds. Maybe I should fool them, type up a couple more stories then hide them in some old magazines...

'What are you smiling at?' Francine asked, as we drank champagne.

I don't know why I told her. It could have been because the champagne had gone straight to my head. More likely I was desperate for someone to confide in. Anyway, I told her the whole thing, gesturing wildly or switching into French if the details got confusing. Francine listened with understanding. She didn't seem to think my imitating Hemingway was pathetic, or deceitful. It amused her.

'A pity I threw the others away,' I said. 'Mind you, Paul was having them tested. He's probably found out that they're fake by now.'

'Why, if the paper was old and the typewriter was old and the ink was old?' Francine asked. She had a point. I poured more champagne.

'This... Helen, are you in love with her?' she asked.

'I don't think so,' I told her. 'She's *tres jolie, mais...*'

'She's too old for you.'

I admitted as much.

'And *tortueux*, too.'

'Maybe. But I think that's more her father.'

'And you are not a *pede*?'

'Philippe thought that was what your father wanted to hear, in case...' I blushed. 'You look very nice tonight.'

Francine blushed too.

We looked at each other and I made up my mind. I'd been thinking of Francine as a girl, but she was nearly a woman. And she wanted me. Yet I hesitated.

'Your parents.' I said.

'They won't be back until very late. Let me show you my bedroom.'

She picked up the champagne bottle and led me upstairs, glass in hand. I am eighteen years old, I told myself. There was something shameful about my still being a virgin. I was a romantic, too. I wanted to be in love with the first woman I slept with. But Francine knew I wasn't in love with her and she didn't mind. Why should I feel bad about it? I finished my second glass of champagne and stepped through the door.

Nine

Pre-twentieth century novelists have a big advantage over those who arrived later. They're not expected to describe sex. There was a time when I got confused reading old books, because a male character would be described as 'making love' to a female character in an almost matter of fact way. After a while, I worked out that, prior to about 1930, 'making love' meant trying to get off with, while, after that date, it meant intercourse. Between the wars, though, you can't be sure what the word signifies, not unless you know what generation the author comes from as well as which generation they are writing for.

Some things are spoilt by putting them into words. This was the first time either Francine or I had been naked in bed with another person. We had all the time we needed. We spent it enjoying each other, edging nearer and nearer to the moment of no return, murmuring sweet nothings. With each new kind of caress, we began laughing like children who were sagging off school for the first time.

The door burst open as I was tearing the wrapper from a condom. Francine's father had been taken ill and come home alone. Concerned that his daughter and I weren't downstairs, M. Gabin jumped to the obvious, correct conclusion. In Francine's bedroom, his face contorted with rage and paternal hurt. Before he could act, Francine jumped between us. Rather than remove his naked daughter, M. Gabin stood back and told us both to get dressed. I babbled apologies in broken French, while Francine protested that we had done nothing wrong, which only made things worse.

Moments later, I was running out of the house, while M. Gabin informed me that, if he had his way, I would be imprisoned, deported, or both. As I ran along the avenue, the street echoed with Francine, announcing to the whole neighbourhood that she was in love with me.

Next day, in our lesson, Philippe advised me to leave the country.

'M. Gabin has connections. He could make life uncomfortable for you.'

'I can't quit my other job,' I told him.

'Then at least change your address. I'm afraid I have to stop coming to you, too. Mme Gabin is my boss. I have to be loyal.'

'According to Francine,' I said, brave now that I'd been sacked, 'she's more than your boss.'

Philippe didn't deny it. 'I hope Francine was worth it,' he said, glancing back as he walked away. 'If she's anything like her mother...' I missed the rest.

I didn't take Philippe's advice about moving house. This was a mistake, because the Sûreté turned up that afternoon and searched my room from top to bottom. They took away the typewriter and my watch, which, they said, matched the description of a consignment that had recently been stolen. I wasn't worried. The typewriter had been bought legitimately and Paul would be able to produce the receipt for the watch when he returned to Paris. I rang the Mercers' hotel and was told that they'd checked out. Not knowing where they were staying didn't disturb me either. I was meeting them the day after next. The Sûreté, meanwhile, advised me to leave the country before they found more charges to throw at me, making dark hints about my indecently assaulting a minor.

The sensible thing to do was leave right away. I didn't need the typewriter in England and I would have had trouble explaining the inscription on the watch. But I was reluctant to give up Helen. She would be back by Sunday morning at the latest. I would wait until then.

Ten

The police hauled me in again in the late afternoon on Saturday. They returned the typewriter, having accepted that the receipt was genuine, but hung onto the watch, which they again questioned me about. Outside, the sky was beginning to get dark when one of the officers produced a photo of Paul, looking ten years younger.

'Do you know this man?'

'Yes, that's him, Paul Mercer.' I hesitated. 'Is he wanted for something?'

One officer murmured something that sounded like 'kidnap'. The other hushed him. Now they questioned me about Paul and Helen, wanting to know everything from what rooms they slept in to how Paul made his money. As I spoke, I realised that Paul paid for everything, not just my services, in cash.

I didn't tell the police I was meeting Helen and Paul the following morning. Nor did I mention the Hemingway manuscripts. It was beginning to occur to me that I was in more than one kind of trouble. First, there was my being caught with Francine. Secondly, my connection with the Mercers might have led me into receiving stolen goods. Thirdly, I was solely responsible for the forging of valuable manuscripts. Tomorrow, I decided, I would tell Helen and Paul where the Hemingway stories had really come from, then get the hell out of Paris.

When the police released me, it was gone eight. I went to a bar I liked, where I drank a couple of glasses of Pelforth Blonde and played pinball until I was nearly in a state of equilibrium. Then I caught the Metro home. There was a note poking out of my door. It read: *I stayed as long as I could. I need to be sure you are safe. You must not call. I will come again tomorrow. I love you. F*

I was touched and a little embarrassed by Francine's final declaration, but her return was the last thing I wanted. The police were looking for the smallest excuse to lock me up. I wrote a note, saying I was sorry, but the police were after me and I'd had to leave Paris. Then I packed my stuff ready for the morning and went to bed.

I slept fitfully, waking at least once every hour, before I drifted into a deep sleep just as I ought to be waking up. It was gone ten when I dragged myself out of bed and dressed, expecting Helen and Paul at any moment. But they didn't come. I made tea, spread jam on dry bread and waited for them. Still they didn't come. By eleven, I was worried. Perhaps they had been arrested. Perhaps they were on the run and couldn't return to Paris. By now I had to get going. I quit my small room for the last time, leaving nothing but the typewriter on which I'd written the note for Francine. In my hurry, I forgot to wedge the note in the door as she'd done with the one for me. She would never find my goodbye where I'd left it, on top of the typewriter I was forced to leave behind.

The flea market was on my way to the Metro, so I looked in. Madame Devonier, the old lady who'd sold me the typewriter, was there again. I asked her if she'd seen a young, attractive American woman with a middle aged man. She had. Helen and Paul had been there at nine, before the market was officially open, looking for very old copies of *Paris Match*. Nobody had had any to sell.

I got out of Paris as quickly as I could.

Eleven

I caught a train to Boulogne, where I took the cross channel ferry, on which I found myself surrounded by boisterous Brits. They were returning from their Easter holidays laden with cheap booze. I felt alienated from this loud, badly dressed crowd, but they left me with nothing to feel smug about. After seven months in Paris, I spoke the language better, but had hardly penetrated the culture. I hadn't made one close French friend, unless you counted Francine, my pupil. Furthermore, in trying to relive the experience of expatriate Americans some sixty years earlier, I'd turned myself into a kind of forger.

I hadn't written to Mum in over a month. She wasn't expecting me back until late July or August. Of late, her letters to me had become briefer, almost guarded. I had no idea why. I took the train to Leam where I splashed out on a taxi. I had the driver sound his horn as we pulled up outside my home.

No-one came to the door. Maybe the library had started opening on Saturday afternoons. I called out as I opened the door, then dragged my heavy bags into the front room, where the day's mail still lay on the carpet. Had Mum gone away? There were no relatives for her to visit. I knew of no old friends who she might go and see. I wondered whether, worried about me, she might have gone over to Paris. How disastrous if we had crisscrossed each other on the channel! But she had been ill when she last wrote and might still be. I went upstairs to her bedroom.

I found her in bed, watching her portable television. Hearing me come up the stairs, calling her name, she was trying to get out of bed in order to hide the damn thing. At first I made a joke of it.

'What's this? Your substitute son?'

Then I hugged her and at once I could feel that she was wasting away. The diagnosis had been suspected before Christmas and confirmed soon after, but she'd delayed telling me, she said, so as not to ruin my time in Paris. Mum was more ashamed of the TV than of her illness, which was cancer. She had, at most, six months to live.

I used to resent my mother for all sorts of things. Not giving me a father, for a start. She wouldn't even tell me who he was. I resented her for not making up a story, which meant that I spent my whole childhood inventing my own: spaceman, soldier, bank robber, millionaire. For a while, I became convinced that my father was the Prince of Wales (Mum had said something nice about him when he was being slagged off on the radio). My best guess was that he had been a student at university. Mum dropped out in her second year in order to have me.

I resented Mum for not having many friends, for being the single daughter of a single mother. Most of the kids around had extended families of some kind. The nearest that I came to an extended family was the other women who worked with Mum in the branch library.

I even resented Mum for not having steady boyfriends. She should, I thought, be bringing blokes home to provide me with a male role model, a stepfather, even. I wanted someone clever enough to impress me and famous enough to impress the kids who bullied me at school.

Most embarrassing, I resented Mum for being what I thought of as poor. Many of the kids at school not only had TVs in their rooms — they wore the latest clothes and went on two holidays a year. I was lucky to get a week in Wales.

All Mum would have had to have done, back when she was nineteen, scarcely a year older than I was now, was to have an

47

abortion. Her life would have taken a different course. She had meant to be a writer herself, or a university lecturer, writing about other writers. Now I was the only vessel for her ambitions. Worse, I had deserted her in her time of need. She had no-one else, her own parents having died when I was a child, too young for me to remember them.

I put my life on hold and determined to make her last days as fulfilled as possible.

Our lives took on a routine. Mum would get up for an hour or two, occasionally leaving the house to get to the corner shop or the doctor's. Then she would move to the sofa, where she would read or I would read to her. There would be sandwiches or soup for lunch. In the evening, I would cook a meal to her directions. During her last months, she taught me to cook, and how to iron, and budget. The house wasn't paid off but she had an endowment mortgage, which meant that, when she died, I would own it outright. This was, she said, her only legacy to me. I told her that this was the least important thing she'd given to me. In that, as in so many things, I was wrong.

After I'd been home a fortnight, I got a letter from Francine. I hadn't left her my address, but she'd obtained it from Mme Blanc at the agency. Francine had got into my room and found the note, so knew that I had not meant to leave without saying goodbye. She had even recovered the typewriter for me. She gave the address of a friend who would act as a *poste restante* and pass my letters on.

I wrote back, glad to unburden myself. I put nothing in my letters that would have caused her parents to blush, while her letters to me were oddly formal, as if she were trying to impress on me how mature she'd become. Perhaps this odd quality was because we both wrote in the other's language, a decision we each made independently. It was as though our lessons were continuing and we were pretending that the bedroom incident had never taken place. Now that our brief clinch was in the past, though, I was glad it had happened, that somebody had wanted me so much. In my miserable mood, I doubted anybody would ever want me again.

Mum slept a lot. During these times, I tried to write, but all I managed were pathetic, rhyming poems and self pitying journal entries. The best periods were when I read to Mum. We read biographies of Sylvia Plath and Daphne Du Maurier, a couple of novels by Graham Greene that she'd never got around to, before rereading her favourite, *The Quiet American*. She requested parts of James Sherwin's strange, psychedelic masterpiece *I, Singer*, as well as new novels by her favourite writers, Toni Morrison and Patricia Highsmith.

The doctor told me Mum's decline had slowed since I came home. I broached the subject of deferring my university place for another year, but she wouldn't hear of it.

Summer came early. For a few weeks, she was able to sit in our small yard while I read to her. Then she was too ill to get out of bed. In August, when they took her into hospital, we both knew that she would not be coming out again.

I cleared the house while Mum was still alive. I wouldn't be able to face doing it once she was dead. I would want rid. Also, though I didn't tell her this, I was looking for some clue to my father's identity. I needed something to do. If I found something, Mum would still be there to explain it to me.

I was still searching for something significant in the clutter on the Sunday morning when the hospital rang to tell me that Mum had died, peacefully, in her sleep, a few minutes before.

Twelve

A small life insurance policy paid the funeral costs and left me enough money to make a start in London. Mum and I had discussed what to do with the house. She thought it would be best for me to rent it out while I was at university. That way, I would have a steady stream of income to supplement my grant. (There were still grants, then, but you couldn't get by in London on a student grant alone.) When I finished my course, I would have a place to live in or a financial cushion to fall back on. I'd gone along with this to keep Mum happy but I meant to sell the house. I wanted to cut all ties with the past and begin a new life in London.

I visited Mum's solicitor, Jon Darkland, in his office. He was a small man, Paul Mercer's age or a little older. But where Paul was ruddy and fleshy, Darkland was lean, with a high forehead and jet black eyebrows. He been mum's solicitor since the death of her parents, not long after I was born.

'Your mother desired that you would rent out the house to provide you with some funds while you attend university. I can advise you on suitable agencies,' Darkland said.

'I think I'd rather sell. I've no intention of returning to Leam.'

'You may be right to do so. The housing market boom can't last forever, while rental demand isn't high in this part of Lancashire. But I should warn you that the proceeds from the house won't buy you the proverbial shoe box in London.'

'Can you put it on the market anyway?'

I didn't want to be encumbered with possessions I would have to deal with later. In the next couple of weeks, as the house went on the market, I sold most of the furniture but for a few basics, then gave Mum's clothes and other stuff I couldn't sell to charity. The things I wanted to keep — a lot of books, two paintings, a few letters and all of the photos — went into boxes in the attic. I would have them sent on to me when the house was sold.

My first term at university did not start well. Despite having more money than the average student, I could find nowhere to stay. After a week in the YMCA, a room came up at a house in Tottenham. I was to share with five second year students, none of whom were doing English or French.

The house was off Philip Lane, with its old-fashioned shops that reminded me of Leam. I was a stone's throw from Broadwater Farm estate, famous for riots a few years before. Unemployment was bad in Leam, but here, at the end of the Thatcher years, seven out of ten adults were unemployed.

At first, I kept my distance from my housemates. I was sure, now I was finally in London that I was bound to meet the literary like minds — male or female — who had been denied me when I was living in Leam. Yet making friends wasn't any easier in London than it had been in Leam. There was a Freshers' week with endless clubs on offer, but none appealed to me. I looked in vain for a society that went to plays or a writing group. University College had no literary magazine. There was a student newspaper, and I offered my services as a reviewer, but the students on the stand said nobody read book reviews and asked if I'd be willing to report rugby games instead.

Other people seemed to get to know each other. They paired off. I went to a Freshers' disco, but it was a meat market. You couldn't hear yourself speak, never mind the person you were trying to talk to, and I was useless at dancing. Spots erupted across my face. I did write to Francine, at her friend's address. I lied, telling her that everything was fine,

London was wonderful, much better than Paris, full of fascinating people. And there were interesting people around. I glimpsed them all the time, people who'd read books, people who I'd have liked to get to know, but I had no idea how to get in with them. For the first time in my life, I was meeting contemporaries who seemed cleverer than me. If I ventured an opinion at odds with theirs, they'd put me right, citing chapter and verse if they were being polite, taking the piss if they weren't.

The ones who impressed me most were an exaggerated, more educated version of the clique members who excluded me at school. They had all been to public schools, some of which had famous names. I sensed that there was a pecking order even amongst them. There were unwritten tests I'd have had to pass before they considered admitting me to the lowest rung of their ladder. I was far too thin-skinned and lacking in confidence to apply for admittance.

While I was cripplingly self conscious, I have to acknowledge some snobbishness too. Looking back, there were offers of friendship that I spurned, though I was barely conscious of doing so at the time. I was quick to pigeonhole some students as boring, not worth cultivating, making the same judgments against them as others used to exclude me. There were opportunities I missed because I lacked the confidence, the common touch, that my contemporaries seemed to take for granted.

Inevitably I started spending my spare time with the people in my house. There were five blokes and one girl, Zoe, who had already paired off with Steve, a Psychology student. The house had no communal rooms, but, since Steve slept in Zoe's bedroom every night, his room became a kind of living room, especially as he had a telly, video and hi-fi. At first we went to the pub a lot, or the cinema, but these cost money, so, by November, we usually ended up in Steve's room.

We all chipped in for beer. As term went on, I chipped in more, because I was the only one with much cash. Steve and Zoe supplied the dope. In Leam, I'd avoided the druggies. Now I became an enthusiastic convert. Smoking hash, I learnt, was a good way of avoiding conversation. None of us had much to say to each other. Steve and Zoe hardly communicated at all. I had least to say, because I had nothing in common with the people I was living with.

I got out of my tree most nights. I made up for the eighteen years I'd spent avoiding television by watching everything, from game shows to soap operas, programmes of which the most that could be said was 'they passed the time'. That was all my time was for, in those days, passing. At the weekend, I liked to drink, only happy when the booze and dope got me to the stage of intoxication where the room began to whirl. If I closed my eyes, I seemed to be in a vortex, dragging me backwards at a hundred miles an hour. I was lost.

Thirteen

My money was going fast. As Mr Darkland had predicted, nobody was interested in buying the house in Leam. Worse, I'd expected to love my course, but hated it. This wasn't because I found it difficult. Old English bored me. Malory's *Morte D'Arthur* left me cold. By the end of the year we'd only be on to Milton. I'd done the first two books of *Paradise Lost* for A level and found it heavy going. I wanted to study twentieth century literature, but there was precious little of it on the syllabus. We wouldn't get to Dickens until the second term of the final year. There were no Americans, unless you counted Eliot, so Hemingway didn't feature.

I was soon behind in my work. I'd made only passing acquaintanceships with other people doing Eng Lit. Few of them seemed interested in reading or writing. Studying stories and poems was an excuse to be in London, not a subject for casual discussion. In the search for allies, I went to the Uni Film club, where I once or twice tried to strike up conversations. I enjoyed going to movies, but didn't know how to talk about them. I knew the titles and plots, not the names of directors or how a particular film fitted in with the rest of their work. Reading novels, I'd learnt to distance myself, to recognise the author's techniques and tricks while, with another part of myself, if the book was good, believing in the story utterly. Films, however, were full of real people. I believed unconditionally in the characters they were playing and tried to identify with them, no matter how unconvincing or inconsistent their behaviour.

I was equally taken in by most people I met. They all seemed so confident, so at home in the world. I assumed they had a fully formed take on life, and I, who hadn't, was the freak. In the Tottenham house, I was the only one who had been to a grammar school. The others went to comps. They teased me if I used erudite words. They mocked culture. Yet I was sure they knew more about life than I did.

In February, I wrote to Mr Darkland, asking him to rent the house if he couldn't sell it. He wrote back saying that this might prove even more difficult in the current climate, but he'd try. I spent less time with the other people in the house. I was short of money for booze and preferred getting stoned on my own, sunk into a book rather than TV.

I read constantly. Rather than be bored silly by the books on the syllabus — who ever learnt anything by reading a book they didn't want to read? — I immersed myself in writing from the sixties, particularly my mother's favourite, James Sherwin.

In March, I got a warning letter from my tutor about missing coursework. He wanted me to go in and discuss it with him. Rather than face this embarrassment, I cut out dope and did the work. As with most things, once I got started, it wasn't as difficult as I'd feared. But my marks were mediocre, barely 2:1 level. I'd always been a high flyer. Now I was one of the crowd.

There was a new problem. Once my money ran low, I became less popular in the house. I had been subsidising the others to some extent. When I stopped rolling endless joints, they had even less reason to be around me. They were home less anyhow. By the middle of the Spring term, all had some kind of job — bar me. I needed one too, but I didn't want to work in a pub or pizza place. There must be jobs that were more interesting, jobs that might lead on to something when I graduated. It might be years before I could earn my living as a writer.

I looked on the Students' Union notice board, toying with medical experiments or becoming a sperm donor. On my third visit, I saw a new ad, neatly typed on the headed paper of the *Little Review*, Soho. 'Sales Rep Wanted'.

I'd heard of the *Little Review*. It was a literary magazine in English that originated in Paris. Hemingway and the poet, Ezra Pound, had their early work published in it. I was surprised to find that it was still going. I waited until the corridor was empty, then took down the ad, so nobody else would see it. Two minutes later, while my nerve held, I phoned the number at the bottom for an interview.

To my surprise, I got through to the editor himself. Anthony Bracken's voice was plummy and slightly camp. He pronounced himself 'delighted' that I wanted to sell the *LR* on campus.

'Come in and see me, old boy,' he said. 'You know where to find us.'

I had never been called 'old boy' before and already suspected there was no 'us'. Otherwise, why would Bracken pick up the phone himself? But I went along to Soho the next day at the arranged time, hopeful of finding the Literary London I had been dreaming of since secondary school.

Fourteen

The *Little Review*'s offices were on a Soho side street that connected the Charing Cross Road with Chinatown. The magazine shared its address with a porn shop. You didn't have to go through the one to get into the other but I wasn't aware of this on my first visit, so ventured shyly inside the Exotic Emporium. I passed stand after stand of glossy magazines in heavy plastic bags. I was the only customer. The bloke who came out of the back had a dyed moustache and a greedy grin.

'You are over twenty-one, aren't you, son?'

'No,' I said, and he looked confused. 'I'm looking for the *Little Review*,' I went on, and his expression cleared.

'Out of the shop, turn right. There's an alley two doors down. Come back on yourself and you'll see a door with an entry phone. If there's anybody there, they'll buzz you in. If there isn't, don't come to me.'

I found the door easily enough, in a dank, urinous recess. I pressed the entry buzzer and there was a long wait. I was about to press the buzzer again when the speaker spluttered into life. A crackly but familiar voice said 'all right, all right, in you come'. The door rattled open and I climbed an unlit, narrow stairwell leading to a shabby door.

'It's open.'

Anthony Bracken was in his sixties, halfway to being bald, and wore a tweed sports jacket that reeked of tobacco — Old Holborn rolling tobacco, I soon discovered.

'Excuse the mess,' were the first words he said to me in person.

I stared at each corner of the large room, which was the size of the shop below, but much fuller. There were pile upon pile of copies of the *Little Review*. The oldest copies were A5 pamphlets with swirling green and grey designs on the cover. Others had arty photographs or cartoons and were of varying sizes, stacked in no discernible order. There was a big old desk, which must once have been quite grand. Its fancy top was a foot deep in papers, except for the cleared space that held a whisky glass and a bottle of Famous Grouse. On each side of the long desk was a tea chest.

'Would you like the full tour?' Bracken said, with a trace of sarcasm.

'Sorry,' I said. 'I wasn't sure what to expect.'

'This was a smart office once. I had two secretaries in the sixties,' Bracken told me, 'Magazine sales paid for one of them, and the other was independently rich, so I didn't need to pay her at all. But times are tight, young man. I can't afford to pay you anything.'

I was taken aback. 'I thought you wanted someone to sell the magazine door to door in halls of residence.'

'That's right. You keep half the cover price. Interested?'

'Yes.'

'Good. You can take a pile away with you. Now, help me sort out this lot.'

And so began my irregular employment at the *Little Review*.

On that first day I helped to tidy the office while the editor went through the tea chest containing what he called 'the slush pile'. The *LR*, he boasted as he skimmed the contents of the brown paper envelopes, was renowned for the speed with which it turned around manuscripts — generally within a week, always within a month. Many other magazines, Anthony told me (somewhere during this conversation he became Anthony, and, by the time I was leaving, Tony) took six months to a year. Because he made a quick decision, people often sent him their best stuff first.

'Here, what do you think of this?'

He handed me a poem by a poet from the provinces whose name I recognised. I read it twice, unsure what to say. I didn't 'get' most modern poems. They were always too difficult or — if I understood them — too simple. But this poet was young and hot. I ought to say I liked it, but could find nothing to admire.

'It's like a well written postcard,' I said, cagily.

'Exactly. He was overrated to begin with and he's already begun to parody himself,' Tony said. 'I can see that you and I are going to get on famously.'

An hour later, I left with a large stack of the last two issues of the *LR* and a book by Graham Greene to review.

'Our greatest living writer,' Tony said, handing me the book. 'I used to see him a lot in the fifties. Published a couple of his stories. He typed them up for me on that desk there while he was waiting for Pepe to be free.'

'Pepe?'

'A tart he was keen on, had a flat two doors down. At first, he used to lie about why he was here. He'd say he had a bit of time to kill. But then, one day, Pepe came looking for him. He'd got wrapped up in something he was writing and she was impatient. Her time was money. Had a biographer round once. Tried to sound me out on whether Graham and I were... you know.'

I didn't, at first, but I nodded sympathetically.

'Just after some dirt. Tarts were Graham's secret penchant, not boys. I didn't let on, though. You aren't that way inclined, are you? Boys.'

'No,' I replied, with an emphatic shake of the head.

'Thought not. Pity.'

Tony was an inveterate gossip, happy to reveal the secrets of famous writers, but he became far more circumspect when it came to his own life. I soon discovered that he had been both a respected poet and a promiscuous gay man in the days before homosexuality was legalised. I liked him a lot, and attributed his weaknesses to circumstance rather than hypocrisy. I wanted to know everything about the prestigious magazine he edited.

On my second day, I asked him about the *Little Review*'s early history, before he was the editor.

'Nothing before me, old boy. I am the progenitor, the one and only.'

'But surely you weren't around in Paris in the Twenties...'

Tony laughed heartily. 'You thought.. well, why not? Different magazine, I'm afraid. There have been several *Little Reviews*. It's a popular title.'

'You copied it?'

'I prefer the word *stole*. Bad writers copy. Good writers steal.'

I recognised his paraphrase of Picasso and remembered how Shakespeare and Co. had stolen the name of the earlier store in Paris. He was right, I decided.

'How did you start?'

'I wasn't much older than you are now. Fresh out of university. A little money from the family. No inclination to get a *proper* job, so I started the magazine as a way of meeting the people whose work I admired. The first issue was mimeographed. Twelve barely readable pages. A hundred copies. Half of them I gave away. The rest I sold, on street corners, going door to door. Writers can be generous to magazines that are starting out. A few gave me good work. A few subscribed. By the third issue, we were folded over, with two staples down the middle, a proper magazine. By the twentieth, the magazine was too fat for staples. We had to have it sewn.'

I liked the way he used the royal 'we' to describe the magazine, even though it had always been a one man band. Now and then, I saw in the old copies I filed, he took on an assistant editor to deal with fiction, art or reviews (he always kept poetry to himself), but the incomers never lasted more than a year or two. Some only lasted an issue. The magazine's sales had peaked in the sixties, but its influence remained strong in the seventies. Since then, subscriptions had dwindled. It was kept going by institutional subscriptions (universities, he explained, paid higher rates and were slow to spot that the zeitgeist had moved on) and paying contributors a pittance. Employing students to sell the magazine, as Tony had in its early days, was a desperate measure. Tony had pinned the notice up himself, in several university buildings. I was the only person who'd responded.

Unloading the magazines was a slog. I didn't possess the natural charm essential for selling door to door. My worthy *would-you-like-to-buy-a-literary-magazine* spiel rarely worked. Often, there was nobody in. I learnt to go round halls of residence just before dinnertime, but was still lucky if I made more in an hour than I would have done working behind a bar. I'd hoped to meet women, but most wouldn't answer the door to a bloke they didn't know and I was never interested in the ones who did. I had an adolescent vision of an instant connection. I was looking for somebody as bright and beautiful as Helen, who liked me as much as Francine did. Yet even if, by some fluke, I'd met such a person, I wouldn't have known what to say to her.

Despite my failure to sell many copies, I began to go to the *Little Review* office once or twice a week. I would help out by filing, answering the phone or taking papers to the post. I liked talking to Tony, pumping him for stories of old Soho. He told me about Francis Bacon, Colin MacInnes, Dan Farson and John Deakin. He took me to drink at the Colony Club and The Caves. These were claustrophobic places full of dodgy types, aging bohemians, aspiring artists and the occasional minor rock star. A few of these people showed a fervent interest in me, at least until Tony warded them off. I thought at the time that I was gathering material for a book (my whole life, I told myself, was merely material I was collecting for a novel). Yet, now that I come to write about that time, I can't recall a single conversation, only snippets, vague images and the occasional cringe-making moment. Tony constantly moaned that Soho was well past its prime.

'The fifties was the time. The blacks were just arriving. Everything was new. Sex. Reefer. Coffee bars. The sixties were a sod, by comparison. The phoneys moved in and the hoi polloi joined up. Things settled down a bit in the seventies. Creeping decrepitude ever since.'

I listened without comment. The fifties and sixties meant little to me, only what I'd gleaned from novels. The seventies were my first decade on earth, though I didn't like to remind Tony of this.

I quickly became Tony's confidante, but I wasn't his only 'helper'. He referred to most of his other acolytes as 'hangers on'. They were twenty- or thirty-somethings of indistinct class, generally shabby dressers, who would offer to take the post or volunteer to review books but rarely did anything useful like hoover or make the tea. Tony warned me that there was one individual who I should never allow to post rejected manuscripts. He suspected him of stealing the stamps off the envelopes and throwing the manuscripts away: 'caused me no end of trouble — half the writers assumed I'd hung onto their stuff in order to use it'.

I learnt to arrive before midday, at which time Tony would often disappear to the Colony Club or one of the other haunts of Soho's daytime drinkers. He let me read manuscripts for him — any that might be of use would join the tottering pile on his desk. Otherwise I would scribble one of Tony's stock phrases at the bottom, then seal up the reject in its stamped, self-addressed envelope. The phrases ran from *sorry, not for us* (complete crap) to *nearly, but not quite there yet* (shows a bit of promise) to *very good, but we've taken too much on at the moment* (a writer who was perfectly competent, or better, but who Tony didn't like). He would sometimes write agonised notes to writers who were evidently his friends. These said something like *tempted to use this, but would be at least two years*. This last was true, he told me, one afternoon, pointing at the tea chest to the left of his desk, which was full to overflowing.

'That's the stuff I've accepted, but haven't got round to using yet.'

When I handed him my Graham Greene review, he affected shock.

'My dear boy, people take review copies to sell. If I really want a book reviewed I give the number of words and a deadline. You should have taken it to one of the places on Charing Cross Road: Henry Pordes or Any Amount of Books.'

Despite this caveat, Tony read my review, marking cuts, correcting the grammar and pointing out places where my point could be clearer, or more succinct. I could see what made him a good editor. The five minutes of attention he gave to my review were more valuable than all the feedback I'd had from the tutor who'd set and marked my undergraduate essays over the previous two terms.

'Here,' he said, handing the review back, 'get it down to five hundred words and I'll try and fit it into the issue after next. If you're interested in Greene, by the way...' He wandered over to the dusty shelves that covered one wall of the room, each one overflowing with books of every hue, in no discernable order. He knew exactly what he was looking for, and where to find it. 'Here. You might want to read this. There could be an interesting article in it.'

He handed me a cheap paperback, published in the 50s, called *To Beg, I Am Ashamed* by Sheila Cousins. Its subtitle was *The Autobiography of a Prostitute*.

'Why?' I asked. 'Is there a Greene connection?'

'Read it first. See what you think. Then I'll tell you.'

The *LR* was a welcome haven, for the house share in Tottenham was becoming unbearable. We were all on the verge of being thrown out. One afternoon in Soho I told Tony that I was badly behind with my rent.

'I suppose you could live above the shop here,' he said. 'I hardly use the place any more. There's only a sink, but you can get a whore's bath in it, and I expect they still have showers at the university. Want a look?'

He took me to the second floor of the building, up the narrow stairs I'd see him climb on days he needed a place to sleep off the drink. There were two rooms. The biggish one had a double bed, a sink, and, behind a shabby curtain, a toilet. The small one was full of tea chests and box files.

'The *Little Review*'s archive,' Tony explained. 'You can clear it up if you want more space. Well, what do you think?'

'It's fantastic,' I, who had always dreamed of living in Soho, said. 'How much rent would you want?'

'No rent,' Tony said. 'You can be night watchman. Sort out the box room while you're here and help keep me organised, the way you have been doing. Oh,' he added, and paused, with a twinkle in his eye, 'and, if I get lucky during the day, the bed still belongs to me. OK?'

Tony never did 'get lucky' any more, though some of his old friends, on finding that I'd moved in, assumed he had. Maybe he did have a kind of crush on me — sex enters most motives, as I had already discovered — but I came to think of Tony as a friend, and even, at times, as a surrogate father.

Fifteen

In Soho, I lived out a fantasy. Many nights I walked the streets, which were most real in the early hours, when there were no tourists. I soon found myself on first name turns with strippers and prostitutes, though conversation was as far as it went: I couldn't lose my virginity to a woman who wanted money in return. As I walked around, I kept making notes, dreaming of the great Soho novel I would one day write. It would be a coming-of-age-in-the-city novel — not a confessional memoir like this, but a sprawling epic, loaded with history, mystery and insight.

The university was within walking distance. My little flat had no stove, so I subsisted on sandwiches, fruit and pot noodles. I'd never been very interested in food, but if I ran out, or was desperate for something hot and filling, there were plenty of cheap Chinese restaurants around. Pollo, a few streets away, served good pasta so cheaply that even I could occasionally afford to eat there.

I read voraciously from Tony's shelves as well as the university library. Few of the novels I read were connected with my course. A degree was merely my excuse for being in London. One of the few non-fiction books I read was *To Beg, I Am Ashamed* the prostitute memoir that Tony lent me. It took me a while to get through, as I kept putting it down, distracted by the more enticing prospect of reading all of Graham Greene's novels, in the order that he wrote them. It was in the fifties, I thought, that he was in his prime. Every novel was even better than the previous one, peaking with *The Quiet American* and *Our Man In Havana*. The prostitute memoir was also published in the fifties. Despite its risqué title, I found the story dull, and easy to put aside. I took to reading it only late at night, when I had finished one book and it was too late to start another.

The book's cover was a silhouetted woman who reminded me more of an underwear advert than the women who worked modern day Soho. The prose was often pedestrian and the story was surprisingly short on salacious detail. Yet I read on, intrigued by the clue that Tony had given me. It was a tale of decline, featuring a weak mother, a missing father, chances not taken and bad luck at every turn. The narrative was populated with seedy men, some of whom could have come from a novel by Greene or Jean Rhys, a thirties writer who my mother liked a lot.

One aspect struck me almost at once. The book claimed to be by 'Sheila Cousins' (at one point, the narrator marries a man called Cousins, who she follows to the far east, one of Greene's favourite locations). Nevertheless, I had read enough books by women to know, almost certainly, that this was written by a man. It was nothing I could put my finger on, just the tone, the choice of detail. It was more than the absence of self pity, the matter of fact attitude to sex. The narrator had none of Jean Rhys's fragility. I realised that for a man to write as a woman was one of the hardest things to pull off. For me to convincingly imitate a female novelist, as I had imitated Hemingway, would be impossible.

A few details in *To Beg, I Am Ashamed* made me think Greene might be responsible for it. Greene's *England Made Me*, written in 1934, had references to selling tea. One of the characters in the novel sent postcards much like the ones sent by "Sheila's" husband, Cousins, when he was in the far east, where he dealt in tea. Sheila drifted in and out of prostitution after her failure to sell vacuum cleaners, a career that Greene used for characters in both *England Made Me* and *Our Man In Havana*, which was written in the fifties. But it was only at the end of the story that she found she had no choice but to remain a prostitute. Then one got the details of the street life, from the three pound punters in Piccadilly (where Sheila worked) to the shilling scrubbers of King's Cross. Greene's regular visits to prostitutes could have been the source of this material.

Most of the writing was humdrum, but now and then the story became gripping, and characters were introduced with telling details. Sheila portrays herself as an intelligent woman who can attract quite distinguished men. Towards the end, she meets an intellectual, a government scientist who falls for her but is put off when he meets a 'dreadful old woman' who he guesses is Sheila's mother.

On his face sat the inhuman solemnity of the stage specialist. Behind every sentence he uttered you felt the weight of an unseen shelf of books.

The tone, the precision of the language, the cadences of the prose and the intelligence of the observation, all of them sounded like Greene — the early Greene, of *England Made Me* anyway. Could Greene have written it under a pseudonym? Why would he bother? By 1953, which was the first publication date given inside the Corgi edition, he was a famous, world renowned author. He didn't need to write a tacky best seller. I noticed, though, that the back of the paperback was taken up by a rave quotation from a distinguished literary magazine, *Time and Tide*. 'I found it deeply interesting, adding to the sum of human knowledge', the review concluded. Who would get a book like this reviewed in *Time and Tide*, a magazine that Greene regularly wrote for, if not Greene himself?

'What did you think?' Tony asked, when I handed back the book.

'There was less about prostitution than I expected,' I told Tony. 'But it held my interest. One thing's for sure. It wasn't written by a woman. Did Greene tell you who it was by?'

'Most people reckon it was written by Cecil Barr.'

'Never heard of him.'

'Wrote a series of racy best sellers in the twenties and thirties,' Tony said, slipping into his gossipy lecture mode. 'His real name was Jack Kahane. He founded the Obelisk Press in Paris. Kahane published people like Henry Miller — writers who English language publishers were far too scared to put out because of the obscenity laws.'

'Did you ever come across him?' I asked.

Tony shook his head. 'He died in 1939.'

'But the book wasn't published until 1950.'

'That was in the UK. I've looked into this. The Obelisk press did a hardback edition in 1938.'

'So this Kahane definitely wrote it.'

'No, Kahane didn't write autobiography. His forte was silly novels. According to Graham, the prostitute book was written by a friend of his, Ronald something, The prostitute was real enough. Both he and Ronald had her. Ronald got a commission to write a book. But he had great trouble coming up with the whole thing and — though he never admitted it, as far as I know — Graham helped him out. The intrigue appealed to him, and the subject matter, of course. He was very circumspect about his dealings with prostitutes. This was an opportunity to make some use of the material.'

'If it was written in the thirties, that makes complete sense,' I told Tony, and recounted the clues I had already spotted. 'Can we prove it? Maybe there's an article about it to be had for the magazine.'

'Maybe,' Tony said, 'but only after Graham snuffs it. He fell out with Ronald, as I recall, and I doubt he'd want to give the book free publicity.'

'Did he tell you which bits he wrote?'

'This was more than thirty years ago,' Tony told me. 'If I'd kept a diary, I'd be quids in, but gossip like that, you only got over a few drinks — more than a few. I can't be sure of any of the details.'

He poured himself another scotch, as though it were medicine that might cure his memory, then ruminated: 'Wish I'd got another story out of Graham back then.'

Sixteen

Within a few weeks, I began to run the *LR* office, a job I loved. It was unpaid but not without remuneration — a rent-free room in Soho was worth a lot, while bookshops on the Charing Cross Road gave me a quarter of the cover price of any review copy I took in. I wrote to Francine, giving her my new address and boasting about my part-time job. She would never have heard of the *LR*, but I had to tell someone, and there was nobody else. She wrote back within a week, asking if I had 'someone special'. (Francine seemed to have a different boyfriend every letter. 'He is not as nice as you,' she would always say.)

I was meeting writers, answering calls from publishers, building up a network of contacts that would one day be of inestimable use, or so I hoped. I was finding out the way things worked. Instead of studying for my first year exams, I spent whole days looking through the archives, putting the house in order, as Tony had requested, in lieu of rent. My first task was to ensure that we had a complete run of the magazine. When this task was complete (only two issues were missing), I began to delve into the box files full of correspondence and old manuscripts.

'Be careful what you do with that,' Tony told me. 'I'm planning to sell the best stuff to American Universities. They're filthy with money, and desperate for authentic papers that have been touched with genius. Don't damage anything.'

'Are old manuscripts really worth that much?' I asked, naively.

'Depends,' Tony told me. 'If the Ms is exactly as published, then it has to be someone really top notch — Joyce, say, or Eliot. But if it's substantially different... here, look at this.'

He handed me the latest *Times Literary Supplement*, folded open at the Random Notes section. I read the following.

Scholars have long debated the fate of the Hemingway manuscripts that were stolen from his wife on a train in Paris in 1922. The thief snatched a briefcase containing every piece of fiction Papa Hemingway had written up to that date. After discovering the loss, Papa was forced to rewrite what he could remember. Serious Hemingway scholars would kill to find these manuscripts, which provide a missing link in the writer's development. Now, out of the blue, one of these stories seems to have turned up in a Paris flea market.

An American businessman was in Paris with his young wife, a Hemingway fan, when they found the story concealed in an old copy of the magazine Paris Match. *With it was a page from another story, never published. On their return to New York, they had the pages examined by forgery experts and Hemingway scholars. Both groups pronounced themselves 'at least 90% certain' that these manuscripts are genuine. The rare papers go up for auction next month. Meanwhile, visitors to Paris will be scouring the flea markets in Clichy, where the Hemingway papers were found, to see if the other missing work (several stories, a novel) is also there. Early estimates say that the newly discovered manuscript could go for as much as two million dollars.*

'Two million,' Tony said, as he put on his jacket to go out for lunch. 'If I ever run out of funds, the contents of that box room are my nest egg.'

Shocked, I nearly told Tony the truth, but didn't know where to begin. I was wary that I might lose my mentor's respect. But I was also proud. My Hemingway forgeries, even the original I thought so weak, had been accepted as 90% genuine.

And so began my accidental career as a forger.

Seventeen

When Tony had gone out to lunch and I'd had some time to absorb the situation, I decided to go to the London Library, at the back of Piccadilly. I didn't know who the American businessman and his wife were. Perhaps Paul had married again or the *TLS* had confused his relationship with Helen. I was sure of one thing. The stories had to be the ones I had written fifteen months before. I already knew the heart of the matter: Helen had betrayed me. How could she and Paul do such a sleazy thing? They had stolen the stories, gone looking for more, then got out of Paris, leaving me to deal with the police.

I didn't belong to the London Library, but Tony did, and he'd shown me around. It was a private library from an age when trust was a given. Their security was so lax, I doubted anybody would challenge my presence. So it proved. I covered a table with recent newspapers. The Hemingway manuscripts started out as a human interest story. All of the accounts began with how Hemingway came to lose the manuscript case. Then, slowly, another tale began to emerge. I followed it at second hand, for the story had first appeared in the *New York Post,* a tabloid that the library didn't take. The details were sketchy at best, for the protagonists weren't giving interviews. It was easy to see why.

Paul and Helen hadn't lied to me, but they had misled me. Helen wasn't Paul's daughter. She was his stepdaughter, the daughter of his second wife. He'd adopted Helen when she was two years old, shortly after marrying her mother. That marriage lasted only three years, but the adoption was never rescinded.

According to the papers, after the divorce, Helen and Paul did not see each other for thirteen years, though Paul contributed to the cost of Helen's upbringing. When she was eighteen, Helen went to university in New York, where Paul (separated from his fourth wife) lived. There — so they had told one paper, though it beggared belief — they fell in love.

Paul's estranged wife discovered they were involved and put a detective onto them. As far as the law was concerned, Paul and Helen were committing incest. The couple had no choice but to run. They fled to Europe, where they planned to stay in hiding until Helen was twenty-one, which was just after our last meeting. As soon as she came of age and Paul's divorce was final, Helen revoked the adoption and married Paul.

No wonder Helen wasn't interested in me. No wonder she couldn't wait to be twenty-one. Back in Paris, I would have been shocked by the relationship, but London had made me more cosmopolitan. The successful writers who stopped by the *LR* offices often had second wives half their ages, while Tony's wealthy gay friends could be found with boys my age or younger. Helen was now nearly twenty-two. Her husband was a little younger than I'd first thought: forty-seven.

At first, I couldn't think clearly. I kept visualising Helen in bed with Paul. I might not be shocked, but I was disgusted. Slowly, it sunk in that the sex wasn't what I should be bothered about. The Hemingway manuscript would set the couple up for the rest of their lives. Unless I exposed them. But how could I do that? I wasn't able to prove that I wrote the Hemingway stories. If I went public with such a claim, there were only two possibilities: the Mercers could say I was lying and it would be my word against theirs, or they could accept that I was telling the truth, but say I had conned them. Either way, I emerged as the bad guy.

Yet why should the Mercers get a couple of million for my handiwork? Here I was, living in a tiny room, my summer term grant already almost spent, my only substantial possession a house I couldn't sell or rent. Surely the Mercers should hand over at least some of the proceeds? The newspaper story speculated about how the stories came to be hidden in those magazines in the flea market. I knew the truth. They never were. However, as far as Helen and Paul were concerned, the stories were my discovery. They must be shitting themselves that I would come forward and immerse them in even more scandal.

One of the American newspapers mentioned which New York hotel the Mercers were staying at. Back at the *LR* office, I took some headed note paper and wrote the couple a guarded letter.

You appear to have sold two manuscripts that belong to me, without my permission. I would be grateful if you would contact me at the above address and explain how you will arrange for me to receive the proceeds of this sale.

I could hardly go to a solicitor. My position was too awkward and, anyhow, I had no money. I thought that using the *LR*'s headed paper would impress them. And it did, though not in the way I intended.

Eighteen

The day after I posted my letter to the Mercers, Tony was in one of his ruminative moods. Lately he'd been going out less at lunchtimes, spending more time on the magazine. I assumed this was because the deadline for issue 498 was coming up.

'Seen a story by Takimoto lying around?'

'No, I'd have read it if I had.'

'Seems he sent me one two years ago. I forgot to publish it. Here.' He handed me a letter from Ken Takimoto, the only author whose every novel had been shortlisted for the Booker prize. Ken pointed out that he had sent Tony a story because he'd received a begging letter saying the *LR* needed to boost circulation if it was to survive, and if Tony wasn't going to use the damn story, he could make a couple of thousand dollars by placing it in *The New Yorker*.

'I suppose it must be in my in-tray,' Tony said, casually indicating the full tea-chest to the left of his desk.

'Do you want me to take a look?' I asked.

'Would you mind? It always depresses me so.'

When he'd gone home, I shut the office and emptied out the tea chest. It was full of papers: letters, CVs, poems, stories, book reviews, memoirs. On each, Tony had carefully scrawled the date of acceptance. Most were from the last year or two. I was discovering what writers tended to refer to as 'the only trouble with the *Little Review*'. While we made quick decisions on whether to accept or reject a piece, Tony was poor at scheduling and frequently took on far more material than he could foreseeably use. For instance, I found an accepted story by Tim Cooper, a writer I'd never heard of, with a letter that was over five years old. In searching for the Takimoto, I found a second letter from Cooper, gushing with joy because he'd had the story taken. The enclosed biog showed that he was twenty-two, a recent graduate. He gave his parents' address because mail at his current residence often went missing.

As I continued going through the pile, I found no Takimoto, but I came across several more letters from Tim Cooper, each detailing a change of address. The letters also contained polite inquiries as to publication date and, finally, an angry plea. His last address was care of a bookshop in Willesden Green. Tony had kept all the letters, but never scheduled the story for publication.

There were similarly petulant or irritated letters from other writers. Had Tony changed his mind about the stories (and, sometimes, poems) but not had the heart to write back? That wasn't in his character. More likely, they had been displaced by a famous name. Authors like Takimoto contributed to the *LR* because it had helped them out early in their careers. In doing so, they expected rapid publication, which inevitably increased the backlog. Occasionally, an impatient author, stuck on the waiting list, would withdraw his or her story, but there was nowhere else as prestigious for an obscure writer to go, so most held on, frustrated.

There were less than a handful of good magazines that regularly published stories by unknowns. A flood of submissions arrived every day. After a few months of sorting the mail, I had learnt to recognise the regulars. They were treated in a cavalier manner, but established writers weren't always treated better, as the Takimoto incident showed. For all I knew, there might be other lost stories by famous authors that Tony had squirreled away on his drunk and forgetful days.

Eventually, near the bottom of the pile, I found Ken Takimoto's story, which was about a widow preparing to go into an old people's home and her inability to commit suicide. It was well written but, I thought, unconvincing. I preferred Tim Cooper's story, an account of a drunken night out in which the narrator learnt some painful, embarrassing truths about himself.

Tony was so delighted I'd found the Takimoto that he took me out to dinner. Issue 498 was late, he said, and he would slot the story into it.

'I'd been thinking of feeding him some line about how I was saving it for the five hundredth issue, but the truth is I can't afford to wait until then. We need a bit of a sales surge at the moment.'

I told him about Tim Cooper's story. 'You've had it for five years. And it's good.'

'Is it? Sometimes I get carried away, or a writer's really persistent.'

I got the impression that Tim's was not the only story that Tony had accepted but never used. 'You have to publish it,' I said.

'Very well,' Tony told me. 'Get him to send an updated biog note. We'll put him in issue 499.'

'There might be a problem there,' I told Tony as our ravioli arrived. 'The last address he gave was a care of, two years ago. He's probably moved since then.'

'If we can't find him, we shouldn't publish,' Tony said. 'We need someone to check his proofs, and there are lots of other people waiting...'

'I'll find him,' I promised, thinking about how I'd feel if I'd written my first decent story and had the thing accepted by the *LR* only for it never to come out.

Nineteen

The bookshop Tim Cooper had given as his postal address wasn't in the phone book. I took the tube to Willesden Green, hoping that it still existed. If I was lucky, somebody there would remember him, maybe even have a forwarding address.

The street took me some time to find. At first, I didn't spot the shop, sandwiched between a greengrocer and a halal butcher. It was a run down, shabby place with a grille in front of the dusty windows, and no name legible above. Only when I got close could I make out that it sold not second hand bicycles or bric-a-brac, but books. A bell rang when I opened the door. Nobody was behind the narrow counter. Shelves stood so close together, there was scarcely room to move. The stock consisted mainly of tattered paperbacks. I found one row of hardback novels, and, in a cluttered back room, a pile of literary magazines, not all of which were in shabby condition. I gave a whoop of delight when I found an old copy of the *LR*. It was one of the two missing from our archive.

'Found something you want?' The speaker was in his mid-twenties, had long hair like mine and wore a plain, grey T-shirt, cheap blue jeans and scuffed trainers.

'Just this magazine,' I told him. 'It's missing from a set.'

The guy looked at the magazine and his eyes narrowed with resentment.

'Fifty pence,' was all he said.

I handed him a coin. 'I'm looking for someone,' I told him. 'He used to live or work here, I think.'

'There's only me and the owner,' the guy told me. 'I've lived in the flat above the shop for a couple of years.'

'Then it must be you I'm looking for. Tim?'

He nodded warily. I spoke quickly, garbling my words. 'I work part time for the *Little Review*, sorting out the archives. I came across this story of yours that should have been published five years ago.'

Tim's eyes became wider.

'Thing is, Tony wants to put it in the next issue and I agreed to track you down so that we can get a new biographical note and send you some proofs.'

Tim still looked angry. 'This isn't a wind up, is it?'

'No, no,' I babbled on about the *LR*, explaining how the issue I'd just bought was missing from the archives and apologising again for the delay in publication. 'Tony was mortified when I told him, but he's incredibly overworked. Mistakes do get made.'

Tim took a deep breath. 'I used to tell people I had a story coming out in the *Little Review*. Then they'd ask to see it.'

'I'm sorry. I know it's been a long time. Have you published much else?'

He listed a handful of small magazines, one of which I'd heard of. 'Nothing that impresses publishers much. I finished a novel, but it didn't quite work. I've started on another one. It's slow going.'

I could see how disheartened he'd become. He was still unsure whether this was some kind of practical joke. 'You'll definitely be in the next issue,' I said. 'If you don't believe me, you can ring Tony, he'll confirm it.'

'That might be a bit uncool. I wrote him a really angry letter a while ago.'

'Two years.' I produced the letter from my pocket. 'If he ever saw the letter, he's forgotten it. As I said, things there are a bit chaotic.'

The letter convinced Tim. 'This calls for a celebration,' he said. 'Fuck it, I'll close the shop. Fancy a drink?'

'If you're buying,' I said. I was skint.

'Sure. But you ought to visit the toilet first.'

This took me aback. But Tim was smiling mysteriously, so I did as I was told, going up some rickety stairs to the smallest room. This was where he'd been when I entered the shop. Immediately I opened the door, I understood why he'd wanted me to see it. Both the walls and the door of the toilet were papered with rejections from publishers and magazines, large and small. There were letters. *Sorry, not for us* wrote the editor of a magazine which advertised that it never rejected material without an explanation. There were comments scribbled on Tim's original letters. *This nearly makes the mark, but not quite,* the editor of *The London Magazine* had written. Mostly, there were anonymous slips. *The editor regrets...We suggest that before submitting more material, you buy a sample copy of the magazine or, better still, a subscription.*

I counted nearly a hundred rejections, many from the same magazine, again and again, the comments changing from neutral to vaguely promising. There were three from Tony, a *not this time,* a *not quite what we're after at the moment* and a *strong work, but we're very full up at the moment* from six years ago. I found rejections from *Ambit, Inkshed, Iron, Panurge, Stand, Slow Dancer, Sunk Island Review* and one I'd never even heard of called *joe soap's canoe. We only publish poetry* the editor of the latter had written, *but if we published prose, yours wouldn't be it.*

Tim had paid his dues. I was seeing, from the other side, what lay ahead for me, if I was serious about pursuing a career as a writer.

In a smoky, side street pub, we drank to Tim's success with the takings from the till. Tim was sanguine about his experiences.

'If you don't have the early years of failure, you're worth nothing,' he said, and I — who had not really tried, never mind failed — agreed. By the time I caught the tube back to Soho, four hours later, Tim and I were bosom buddies.

Back at the office, I put Tim's story in the file to go to the typesetter, then put his biographical details and address in the folder marked 'recent correspondence'. The top drawer of Tony's desk, usually kept locked, was half open. This was where he kept personal correspondence. But the letter on top of the scattered heap was hardly personal. It was from the London Arts Board.

The letter was short and to the point, stating that the *LR*'s circulation had fallen to such a level that the size of its Arts Board grant could no longer be justified. It went on to say that there was great competition for grant money from other magazines. Unless the *LR*'s circulation doubled by the end of the year, the board would have no choice but to reduce the grant level substantially. I read the letter twice then pushed the drawer shut.

The *LR* was on the verge of going bust. I shouldn't have been surprised, but I was. Tony took no money out of the magazine. He lived off a state pension supplemented by money from poetry readings and occasional journalism. Until his parents died, in the seventies, he'd lived either with them or in the tiny flat that I now occupied. He'd moved up in the world, but often complained about the rates on the flat he'd inherited in Highgate. With a reduced grant, Tony wouldn't be able to afford to pay contributors their already tiny fees. He might not be able to pay the printing bill. He badly needed to find a way to boost circulation.

That night, I couldn't sleep for worrying about the magazine going under. My whole future seemed bound up with it. One short story from a famous writer wouldn't be enough to lift sales. Tony needed several, soon. He might be able to beg one or two, but I had learnt that big name writers don't keep masterpieces hidden in their bottom drawers, saved for a rainy day. Nor could most of them come up with a new story at short notice.

There was, however, somebody who could make up stories quickly, who could imitate the style of other writers and pass them off as genuine. Somebody who owed Tony a favour. He could, maybe, if he tried hard enough and chose well, single-handedly save the magazine. For, if I could forge Hemingway and fool experts, why shouldn't I be able to forge someone else just as convincingly?

Who? I had been working on my own fiction all this time, writing either autobiographical wallowings that I destroyed the next day or surreal, semi-mythical nonsense that I kept, but never showed to anyone. I had no enthusiasm for my own writing. I did not believe in myself. This new project, how-ever, fired me up. I began looking through the LR's archives, neglecting my university work to search for ideas.

At first I thought the ideal author would be somebody who had contributed to the LR in the early days and since died, leaving only a small body of work. But there was a problem with that. Many authors suffered a slump in sales in the decade or two after their death. The forgee had to be some-one whose work I loved, and could immerse myself in. My first thought was JD Salinger. I reckoned I could easily imi-tate the style of *The Catcher in the Rye*. But I soon decided against this. Salinger was already much imitated, and the men-tally disturbed, over clever, over educated Salinger characters reminded me too much of myself. Also, Salinger hadn't pub-lished anything new in nearly thirty years. He'd recently sued a British poet who tried to publish a biography of him, so he was certain to sue anyone who published a story without permission. I wanted to save the *Little Review*, not bankrupt it.

My next thought was James Sherwin, nowhere near as famous as Salinger, but still a cult and, I thought, a more interesting writer. Sherwin had published less than Salinger, and had been absent for almost as long. Moreover, two of his stories had been published in the *LR* in the early sixties. I'd found the Ms. of one of them, a story that later appeared in his only collection, *User*. Sherwin's big success came with *I, Singer* in 1967, then there was the book of stories and a novella, *Stargazer*, in 1970. Nothing since. My mother had a signed copy of the last book.

I remembered Mum telling me how, as a student, she saw Sherwin give a reading. He read from *Stargazer*, then from another, as yet unpublished and unfinished book, *A Commune*. After the reading tour, Sherwin returned to his Greek island, which he hadn't left since, to complete his magnum opus. *A Commune* was talked about for years. People who'd heard Sherwin read extracts declared that it was going to be 'the novel to end all novels'. Sherwin — still only in his late thirties — said that *A Commune* would be his final novel: he'd said in it all that he ever wanted to say. Only the book never came out. Nor did anything else.

Sherwin's three other books remained in print but were out of fashion, except with old hippies and a certain kind of student. Nevertheless, an *LR* containing a new story by him could quadruple its print run and still sell out. The only drawback I could see was this: Sherwin had published so little that he was unlikely to have forgotten a story sent out when he was a young man. Even if I could get a letter to Sherwin and convince him that he'd written a story and forgotten about it, I still had to write the story. And that wouldn't be easy. From the start, Sherwin's world weary style was unique. There were hints of Borges, even Nabokov, yet he was also English. His subject matter drifted from working class life in the Midlands to a semi-mythical, ascetic world. He was fascinating, but would be very hard to fake. I needed someone easier. Preferably, someone who was dead and couldn't kick up a fuss.

The answer only hit me as I was walking through Soho, more intent on my lunch than literary forgery. In the window of Any Amount of Books was a first edition of one of my mum's favourite novels, Graham Greene's *The Quiet American*. Greene had started me thinking about faking a living writer. He had contributed a story to the *Little Review*, typing it up in the office while waiting for his female friend to be free. If he had typed up one, why not two?

There was a problem with forging Greene. He was still alive. But, recent reports indicated that he had a poor memory. The previous year, a novella of his, written to be filmed thirty years ago, had been found in a drawer in Hollywood. It had been published, to wide acclaim, as *The Tenth Man*. Greene said he had no recollection of writing it. ('He was taking a lot of Benzedrine at the time,' Tony commented.) *The Tenth Man* wasn't the only example of his dredging up forgotten work from the far past. One of his late seventies novels, *The Human Factor*, was something he'd started in the early sixties, then abandoned.

Since then, the novels had dried up. His last book, the one I reviewed, was a selection of his letters to the press. He was about to publish a thin collection of stories, *The Last Word*, which, the accompanying press release said, contained work written between the nineteen twenties and nineteen eighties. Two of the stories in it had been published in the fifties and not seen since. Why would anyone doubt the credibility of another previously unpublished story from that era?

Back in my room, I was slowly clearing out the box room to make space for my own stuff. There were boxes full of what

Tony called the *LR* archive, but there was also plenty of rubbish. Amongst the debris I'd found a broken toaster, an early electric kettle and an old typewriter. I'd thrown out the first two but kept the latter, because it reminded me of the typewriter I'd left behind in Paris. Now it occurred to me that this might be the typewriter that Greene used to write his stories on all those years ago. The typeface looked similar to the manuscript in the archive. The typewriter ribbon was useless, but I would track down an old one somehow, if I managed to come up with a convincing story.

That night, as the Soho streets grew noisy beneath me, I sat at Tony's desk, as Greene had done thirty odd years before, and began to write.

Twenty

When I tried to come up with ideas for stories of my own I found it impossible. Yet, when I impersonated Graham Greene, it was hard to hold back my imagination. That didn't mean I could write a convincing forgery. Much of what I'd read was set abroad. Too risky to write about a place I'd never visited. One wrong detail and I would be exposed.

I remembered a line from Meyer's biography of Hemingway: *the truth about a man is what he hides.* Tony had passed on a similar piece of advice, given by a friend who'd spied during the war: *if you want to know a person's weakness, find out what he lies about.* What did Greene lie about? Cheating on his wife? Hardly. His affairs were common knowledge. But going to prostitutes was seedier. That was something he might disguise in his fiction. Major Jones in *The Comedians* confesses to the narrator that he's never had a woman he hadn't paid for. How often did Greene pay for it?

I began a story about a prostitute. I wouldn't include it here, even if I could. When you look at a forgery, knowing it to be a forgery, its faults are bound to be immediately apparent. Whereas if you read it wanting to believe or, better, needing to believe, that's a different matter, as the success of my Hemingway forgery showed.

In *A Girl He Used To Know*, Sedgeworth, a forty-something jeweller with a dying, disabled wife, sees a young prostitute in Soho and, although he's never used a prostitute before, feels compelled to sleep with her. The prostitute, who calls herself Eve, commutes from Nottwich, the fictional city that Greene based on Nottingham. Nottwich first appeared in the thirties novel *A Gun For Sale* and is mentioned in *Our Man In Havana*, which was written during the period when my story was set. Nottingham was where Greene started out as a journalist, before getting a job on *The Times*. He hated the place, but his few months there gave Greene his only taste of working class life. It was an experience that seemed to have stuck with him. In my story, Sedgeworth had lived in Nottwich for a short time when he was starting out, giving him a connecting point with Eve.

There is something about Eve that keeps drawing the jeweller back. She is not a classic beauty: her jaw is too square, her shoulders a little too wide. She is not sexy or glamorous enough to work the classier sections of the metropolis. Sedgeworth, she says, is her favourite client. They talk easily and become affectionate. He finds himself falling in love with her. He even tells Eve about his dying wife, who, he says, probably suspects that he is seeing someone, but would never ask. Eve tells him that she does not intend to be a prostitute forever. She wants to open a dress shop, one that also rents outfits to those who don't want, or can't afford to buy. Sedgeworth offers to be her guarantor. After some hesitation, Eve agrees. At this point, she tells him her real name, Hannah.

Sedgeworth plans to set Hannah up as a respectable, independent woman of business. When his wife dies, after a suitable interval he will be in a position to marry her, but only if she will have him. In the meantime, Hannah will escape prostitution, and he will remain her lover.

Hannah tells Sedgeworth that she never knew her father, who died before she was born. One day she would like him to meet her mother, who she is very close to. It would be safest to introduce him as her backer, rather than her lover, as her mother has no idea what she really does in London. Later, when his wife dies, the couple can say that their romantic relationship began shortly afterwards. Sedgeworth agrees to this charade.

I already had too much plot for a short story, I realised, though not enough for a novel. People would assume that this was why Greene didn't proceed with the piece. After working out the ending, I pared the piece down and practised Greene's metaphors. Greene's wife, Vivien, used to go through his work, removing what she called 'tigers in the woodpile', that is, overblown imagery that cheapened the story. I did the same.

There were other details I had to get right. I found a ribbon that more or less fitted the old typewriter, though it slipped occasionally. There were plenty of blank sheets of manuscript paper scattered among the papers in the archive, and it was easy enough to find a dozen that seemed to match. Indeed, I was left with a number of spares, which I would put to good use in due course.

Only when I was very sure of what I had written did I get out the old typewriter. I copied the piece out, making the odd improvement as I went along, taking care to use the same layout as Greene in the genuine story I'd seen.

When I was done, I left my story spread out by a window for a couple of days, hoping the sun would age it. Ten days after I'd begun, I read the story again. Finding no errors, I took a deep breath, then went down to show it to Tony.

'Where was this?' he asked as he glanced at the Ms..

'In an unmarked box-file upstairs.'

'Which issue was it in?'

'It was never published. I checked the index.' (An index of the *LR*'s first two hundred issues had been published in the 60s.)

Tony took the story to read on the old leather armchair in the corner, shifting a pile of books so that he could sit there. I dealt with the minor correspondence, making as little noise as possible. From time to time, I glanced in his direction. Had

I got the ending right? As the shop opens, Sedgeworth's wife suddenly dies. He is free to be with his mistress. But when he turns up, unexpectedly, to tell Hannah the news, her mother is there on a visit. Hannah introduces Sedgeworth as her sponsor. The mother, who is Sedgeworth's age but beaten down and dishevelled, is warm with him and exhibits no suspicion of his motives. Sedgeworth is sure she will accept his marrying Hannah. He can't wait to get his mistress alone so that he can tell her his news.

But it's the mother who manages to get Sedgeworth alone. While Hannah is downstairs, seeing a customer, her mother hugs Sedgeworth, and tells her how grateful she is to him. But how, she wants to know, did he find out about Hannah? James Sedgeworth has no idea what she means. I didn't know how to contact you, Jim, the mother tells him. How did you know she was yours?

Sedgeworth at last understands. Hannah's mother is a factory girl he had a brief fling with twenty-three years earlier. Her daughter is also his. Perhaps the filial resemblance is the reason for his tremendous attraction to her.

'You were always a gent', the mother tells him, as he bluffs his way through the situation.

James and Hannah see the mother to the train back to Nottwich. As they leave St Pancras, James Sedgeworth tells Hannah that his wife needs constant attention. He will not be able to visit his lover for a long time. He wants her to see other men. Hannah is hurt and confused. Sedgeworth leaves her at the station, in tears. In the last line, he returns to his empty house.

Tony put down the story.

'I don't remember this at all,' he said, shaking his head.

'Perhaps he didn't show it to you?' I ventured.

'No. He used to talk to me about Pepe, that was the girl's name. Why shouldn't he show me the story? Unless he changed his mind about it. This is a brilliant find, Mark, but I'm going to have to contact Graham before we schedule it. I'll get it photocopied tonight, write him a note.'

Tony smiled and settled down to reread the story. I went back up to my room with a sense of anticlimax. I was meant to be studying for the exams that started the next day. The typewriter I'd written the story on was still by my bed. I returned it to the box room, replacing it with the Amstrad word processor my mum had bought me for my sixteenth birthday. I half expected Tony to come in at any moment, tell me the Greene story was a fake, and throw me out of the flat. But he didn't. The next day, he told me he'd written to Greene.

'Fingers crossed,' he said.

I was sure I'd made a huge mistake, one that Greene would quickly expose.

Twenty-one

My first year exams were a disaster. I hadn't taken them seriously, being far too wrapped up in working for the *LR* and preparing the Graham Greene story. The exams didn't count towards the final degree mark. You only had to pass to get through to the next year. So I'd slacked. I'd long since stopped attending lectures, but I'd gone to most tutorials. I'd studied one of the core texts at A level and felt I knew it inside out. But A level was two years ago and I had never got to grips with old English, or Malory. I was a hot shot at Twentieth Century stuff — hadn't I convinced experts that I was Ernest Hemingway? But we didn't get to the modern era until the Third Year. I hadn't put in the donkey work on the syllabus. I left my last, three hour exam an hour early, because I couldn't think of a single thing more to write. The prospect of failure terrified me.

When I got back to Soho, Tony handed me a letter that had come in the second post. It was postmarked New York. The handwriting was a scrawl, but I recognised its author, and went upstairs to read it, much to Tony's amusement.

Helen Mercer was replying to my letter, which had been addressed to her husband. She pointed out that she and Paul had had no way of finding me until now. Helen was, she said, coming to London to see me 'as soon as proves possible'. There was no mention of money, nor of whether Paul would accompany her.

Graham Greene also replied quickly. Tony read his letter to me. In it, Greene said that he had been ill since a trip to Dublin the previous year, and was about to move from Antibes to an apartment in a small village called Corseaux, which had good views of Lake Geneva and the Alps.

'Doesn't say why he needs to move,' Tony commented.

'Probably to be by a hospital. It must be more serious than he says, poor sod. Listen to this'.

> *Thank you for sending* A Girl He Used To Know. *I have no recollection of writing this story, though I do, of course, recall the circumstances that gave rise to it. Pity it's too late to put it in* The Last Word. *Whatever happened to poor Pepe? All in all, not a bad inversion of the Greek myth. Use it if you think it's up to scratch and thank you for the invitation. I regret that ill health does not allow me to visit London — or elsewhere — as I would like. All good wishes, yours ever, Graham.*

He had returned the photocopied typescript with two minor amendments, improving the style in one place, removing an unnecessary comma in another. Tony was cock-a-hoop. I restricted myself to a gratified smile.

'We'll carry it in the next issue, pull that story by what's-his-name.'

'You can't do that,' I said. 'I promised Tim his story would be in issue 499. Wouldn't it be better to hold the Greene for the five hundredth issue?'

Tony gave me a wary look, but didn't argue about dropping Tim's story.

'No,' he said. 'We need the sales that the Greene will give us now. With luck, you'll find something else in the archives that we can use in number five hundred. And I'll write to a few of our regulars, ask for a special contribution. I'll print extra pages, pull half of the review section, whatever's necessary. But I want it out soon.' His eyes brightened, and he added, 'we'll have a launch party. That'll show we mean business. It's years since we had a launch party.'

Tim came round that evening. I told him about the launch party.

★★★

'Tony would like you to read your story. Would you do it?'

'Would I?' Tim was very excited. He confessed he hadn't done any work on his novel all year, but the news of impending publication had spurred him into action. 'I've written five thousand words since you appeared last week! I'm usually a slow writer, but I reread what I'd done so far and all of a sudden, it made sense — I know what needs changing, where the book's going.'

Tim was fascinated by the *LR* offices. He was so enthusiastic that I showed him my upstairs quarters, where he spent half an hour digging around in the box room. As he left, Tim offered to help me with the archive work, but I told him that he should spend his free time writing.

Tim's friendship affected me greatly. I had found a companion who, while a few years older than me, was still in his twenties. He was the first person I'd met of my own generation who also wanted to be a writer. I felt a little less lonely. I even had another go at my own fiction, although I knew that there was a more pressing need. Tony was counting on me to discover another 'lost' story in the archive for the *Little Review*'s five hundredth edition.

Twenty-two

The exam results were posted on a notice board near a lecture theatre I hadn't been inside since the Autumn term. By the time I found it, there was no crowd, which saved my blushes. I had always been able to coast before. I'd known that I'd done badly, but figured that I would get through and could improve my grades later. It was too late. I'd failed.

My tutor was in his office. The resigned cordiality with which he let me in suggested that he'd been expecting me. My file was on his desk. The university was run in such a ramshackle, anonymous way that it hadn't occurred to me until then that I even possessed a file.

'You've got no excuses, Mark,' he said. 'Your attendance at lectures has been the worst in the year.'

Nobody had told me how, once the numbers began to fall, lecturers routinely passed round an attendance list. That was what happened when you failed to make friends in your year.

'You've missed three out of your twenty tutorials with me and you've often come under prepared.'

There was no denying this.

'You walked out of your most important exam an hour early, having failed to complete the paper. Nobody's going to be generous in their marking when they hear stories like that.'

I hung my head. I had thought myself unnoticed, virtually anonymous, but all the time people had been making notes on me. There was no coming back, that was what my tutor was telling me.

'What surprises me,' the tutor went on, 'is that you came with such good references. Excellent A level grades. You're described as loving literature, as having a vocation to be a novelist. Is that what you've been doing these last few months, writing a novel?'

I shook my head. I didn't have the energy to lie. Anyway, he might ask to see it.

'Your mother's a librarian, it says here. How's she going to take this news?'

In disbelief, I looked at his expression. Was he taking the piss? But why should the University know that my mother had been dead for nearly a year? I hadn't told them.

'Are you all right, Mark? Pull yourself together, lad.'

The tutor handed me a tissue because I was blubbing like a baby.

Later I was told that, given my bereavement, I would be allowed to return and retake my exams the following year. If I passed, I could continue my degree as if nothing had happened (though I would, for the first time in my life, be older than most of the people in my year). Presuming that I managed to support myself in London during my year off, I could even drop in on the lectures I'd missed.

My mother had helped me again. Although she had been dead for ten months, her absence affected me more than I would admit to myself. I was in a numb state that partly explains the way I behaved. I didn't think of myself as an adolescent, still less as an orphan. But I was both. Maybe I still am.

I returned to Soho chastened, yet relieved. I wasn't ready to be a student. There were things I had to do first, not least restoring the *Little Review* to its former fortunes. If the Mercers didn't come through with some money, I would have to get a job, but that decision was way off in the future.

I told Tony that I was taking a year off from university and would like to spend more time on the magazine.

'Is that possible?' he asked, but didn't hint that he knew the real reason. 'I'll tell you what,' he said. 'I'll see if I can scrape up some work for you.'

'It doesn't matter,' I said. 'I can sign on in the summer.'

'You'll need to do that too,' Tony told me, with a sad smile.

The 499th issue of the *Little Review* came back from the printers two days before the launch party. It had a black and white photo of Graham Greene on the front with the words, 'Greene: A Major New Story' in white lettering, reversed out over a dark Soho street. Tim's name was also on the cover, listed alphabetically in the 'new stories and poems by...' strip at the bottom.

Tim was first to arrive at the party, which took place in Turret Books on Lamb's Conduit Street. He'd had a haircut for the occasion. I realised for the first time that he was handsome, in a foppish, almost feminine way. Second to arrive was Magneta McLaren. It was the first time I'd met Magneta, whose bizarre, sententious short stories were published by the *LR*, *Ambit* and several other magazines. She was thirtyish and heavily made up in goth style, with a shock of black hair and a gold studded nose. Magneta wore a tight tank-top and blue jeans so full of holes that it was impossible not to notice the absence of underwear. Recognising her from Tony's description, I introduced myself.

'Where have you been hiding?' she wanted to know, then pinched my bum with a playful grin. 'You're not a fag, are you?'

As I fumbled for an answer, Tony emerged from the back room, where he had been conducting some kind of negotiation with the bookshop's owner.

'Magneta, my dearest!' He managed to extricate her from me, then whispered in my ear, 'you'd better watch out, Mark,

Magneta likes them young. She'll have your cherry in no time if you let her.'

'Who the hell was that?' Tim asked, as more people arrived. I told him.

'Magneta McLaren!' Tim was impressed. 'She was in the Granta "Thirty under Thirty" issue.'

'Do you like her stuff?'

Tim didn't answer. He was staring at Magneta's backside. From what he'd told me, it was years since he'd had a steady girlfriend. Few self respecting women would sleep with a man who wore cheap clothes, had a lousy job and lived in a dusty bedsit above a secondhand bookshop. When Magneta was obscured by new arrivals, Tim and I talked about the new issue. He's already read it, cover to cover.

'Just to see what company I'm in.'

Tim was kind about my Greene review, but reserved his enthusiasm for my forgery.

'That Greene story,' he said, 'it feels really fresh, not like something from the fifties at all. You know, when he asked about her mother, and worked out...'

I listened spellbound as, for five minutes, Tim talked about *A Girl He Used To Know*. It was one of the most flattering, intense conversations of my life. He had found one or two flaws, but linked the story to aspects of the author's life that I hadn't even considered. He picked up a copy of the magazine and quoted my own words at me. It was all I could do not to jump up and down announcing that I'd written the thing myself. Magneta came over with a glass of wine for me.

'I saw you were empty.' Then she noticed Tim's rapt interest in her and asked if he wanted another drink.

'Better not yet,' he said. 'I'm meant to be reading in a few minutes.'

All of Magneta's attentions switched from me to Tim. 'Oh,'

she said, picking up a copy of issue 499 from the display table. 'So you're...'

A few minutes later, Tony introduced Tim to the thirty or so people who had crowded into the narrow space. He apologised for Graham Greene's absence, going on to say how he was sure that Graham would have deferred to important new talent like the young man who was about to read.

'As soon as I began Tim's story,' he said, oozing sincerity, 'I knew we had to have him in the *Little Review*. He's one of the freshest voices I've come across in years. But don't let me ramble on, listen to him for yourself. Tim Cooper!'

I hadn't been to many readings during my nine months in London, so I had little to compare Tim with. I'm pretty sure, though, that he was terrible: hesitant, incoherent at times, stressing words in the wrong place. He had no sense of timing. If I hadn't already read the story, I'd have thought it was rubbish. As it was, I doubted my judgment. Yet, when he was through, people clapped enthusiastically, as though Tim had completely justified Tony's introduction of him. Magneta, especially, looked bowled over.

'What did you think?' Tim asked me.

'You sounded somewhat... nervous.'

'I was scared shitless. I should have got drunk first, I couldn't have been worse. Nobody laughed at the jokes, did you notice?'

'They're an odd audience,' I said, looking round, and they were. Badly dressed, anorexic or overweight. Most were getting on a bit and drinking as though prohibition was about to be introduced. We were the only guests in their twenties. It was hardly the Literary London I'd dreamt about. According to Tim, that was happening half a mile away, where magazine writers ten years my senior snorted cocaine in the toilets of a trendy club, then babbled about the novels they had already been commissioned to write. I'd read about these people and knew where to find them. I also knew that they wouldn't be interested in me — at least, not until I was 'someone'.

People wanted to talk to Tim, so I drifted away, pleased that my new friend was enjoying his success, but wishing there were publishing people present for Tony to introduce him to. The days when agents and publishers would scour the *LR* for new talent were long gone, but you never knew — somebody influential might buy the issue for the Greene story, come across Tim's piece and fall for it.

I had another glass of wine and brushed against Magneta. Alcohol has always affected me quickly. Now that I was intoxicated, Magneta looked even more attractive.

'I liked your friend's story,' she said.

'Yes, me too.'

'I like your friend,' she went on, with a charitable shrug, making it plain I wasn't in with a chance. Tim joined us. A few words of praise from Magneta and he started gushing. To distract myself, I began to collect glasses. The booze had run out, so the crowd was rapidly thinning. I took two handfuls of glasses to the tiny kitchen. Then I rejoined the party and looked for Tim. He appeared to have already gone, which was strange. I noticed that Magneta had left, too.

'I think she persuaded your friend to walk her home,' Tony told me, as he began to clear up.

Soon after, Tony left with one of his old boyfriends. It seemed he, like Magneta, was on a promise. Alone, I carried unsold copies of the magazine back to the *LR* office, walking hunchbacked, unnoticed, through wide, emptying streets, reflecting on the rewards that my career in forgery had reaped so far. I'd felt invisible all my life. I thought that writing was a way of making myself real, but so far it had only made me more invisible.

By faking the Greene story, I might have helped to keep the *LR* going. But that was a selfish act, not an achievement to be proud of. It meant I had a roof over my head and something to occupy my days.

Suppose — just suppose — I'd published the story under my own name, and Tony had accepted, published it? Maybe I'd have been the one who Magneta McLaren took home that night. And everything that followed might have been prevented.

Twenty-three

Much of the next month was spent squashing magazines into pale brown jiffy bags and hauling large piles down to the post office. A few weeks later I saw the bookshop returns figure for issue 499. There were none. We'd upped our print run to 4,000 and the issue still sold out. Subs were up too. If we got a similar sale for the 500th issue, the *LR*'s future was secure and it wouldn't matter if I never saw a penny for the Hemingway stories that Paul Mercer had apparently made so much money from. I put that problem to the back of my mind. The important thing was that, if I passed my retakes, I could return to university the following autumn, knowing that my year off had not been wasted.

I had another challenge to face before I returned to academic work. Tony needed a story as the centrepiece for the five hundred issue, which was going to be a double size, anniversary edition.

'The best ever!' Tony announced to anyone who visited the office. 'Jim Ballard's promised a story. Spike Milligan and Ted Hughes are doing poems. Bill Burroughs says he'll come up with something.'

In other words, none of the above had actually delivered their material yet.

'I've even written to James Sherwin,' Tony told me.

'Really?' Since finishing the Greene, I'd been working on a story that was a kind of homage to Sherwin, drafting and redrafting it on my cheap word processor. What a coup it would be if Tony came up with the real thing!

'No reply as yet. Now, what have you got for me?'

I was silent.

'You've been trawling through the archives, I take it?'

'I haven't gone through the really early stuff yet,' I said. 'It's in a bit of a mess.'

'Seen this?'

He held up an obituary of Roald Dahl from that day's paper. 'I published him just after he started out. 1950, it must have been.'

'I hadn't noticed that,' I said.

'Don't suppose we put his name on the cover. He wasn't my kind of writer. But I could tell he had something. I very nearly used another story by him, shortly afterwards. I can't recall why I didn't, it's so long ago.'

When Tony went out to lunch, I read the obituary. After a series of awful tragedies in his life, Roald Dahl had become one of the century's most successful children's authors. His previous work for adults was quite different. I hadn't read him for ten years, but remembered his style as plain but witty. There was a darkness in his work that appealed to children. The same thing looked immature in his adult work, or so I thought at the time. Had an old Dahl story survived in the archives? From what I'd seen, Tony had been more organised in the fifties than he was now. We might get lucky. But it was unlikely. Putting aside the pile of manuscripts to deal with, I dug out the magazine containing the one Dahl story the *LR* published, from early 1950. Then I went into the box room.

One end of the room contained neatly stacked files, the fruits of my endeavours so far. The other held half a dozen decrepit tea chests, piled high with the detritus of the magazine's first twenty years. I had barely explored these, beyond digging out the Graham Greene manuscript whose lay-out I had copied for *A Girl He Used To Know*. The chests were, at least, labelled. With difficulty, I lifted the chest containing 1962-66 and put it on the ground. Then I sat on it while I explored the first box, 1947-1951. Here were the original manuscripts of all the stories, articles and poems Tony had published. This was the most valuable box, I supposed, Tony's nest egg, destined, perhaps, for the University of Iowa, or Texas. I ought to have worn gloves as I looked at them.

Tony's handwriting as a young man was more rounded, less spidery than now. His organisation was better, too. The original manuscripts, together with the correspondence from each issue, were contained in clearly labelled foolscap envelopes. It didn't take me long to find the Dahl story, together with a letter from the author. But that was it. I went through the envelopes containing later issues. Tony had kept very little relating to work not published. If Dahl had written to him, offering another story, the letter was long gone. But so what? The story might have existed. It could still exist, if I wrote it.

I sat down at my computer. I cleared my mind, then set about pretending to be Roald Dahl. It couldn't be more difficult than becoming James Sherwin, which I'd been working on until then. Dahl's adult fiction was mainstream, part of a tradition that came out of Somerset Maugham and other upper middle class scribblers. The difficulty was in coming up with a story idea. In my old student house, I'd watched *Tales of the Unexpected*, a series based on his stories. I knew about twists in the tale, but had no idea how to come up with an original one, like the police investigators eating the leg of lamb that, when frozen, had been the murder weapon.

I wrote a couple of opening sentences, then a complete paragraph that sounded authentic. But no story came. I locked the office and headed off to Charing Cross Road, looking for a secondhand edition of some early Dahl stories. Should I came up with an idea, I would still need a way to forge the Ms. I had no idea what make of typewriter Dahl used. All this was weighing on my mind as I turned into Any Amount Of Books and bumped into Tim and Magneta.

The couple were hand in hand and so absorbed in each other they didn't notice me until I spoke their names. Tim appeared embarrassed.

'I'm sorry I haven't been in touch, Mark. It's just that we...'

'I understand,' I said. 'How's the writing going?'

'Fantastic. Magneta persuaded me to give up working in the bookshop. I've moved in with her.'

'Great.'

'We wanted to have you round...' Tim began.

'Come tonight,' Magneta interrupted. 'Tim tells me you write. You must bring some of your work. We'd love to hear it.'

'I don't know. I...' But Magneta was already scribbling her address on the back of a paper bag from the herbalist's up the road.

'About nine,' she said. 'I'll cook.'

Tim gave me the look of a man in the grip of an irresistible force and they set off. Within an instant they were, again, completely wrapped up in each other.

I found an old copy of Dahl's *Switch Bitch* in Henry Pordes Books and took it back to the flat to read. Winter was slow in leaving and the flat was very cold. I had lost weight. Maybe a meal out would do me good.

The book I'd bought was a tatty hardback, much read. I could have bought a pristine secondhand paperback for the same money, its pages already discoloured and brittle even though they had never been read. But I had a penchant for used books and hard covers, for reading a book as it first appeared. This one's original owner would be dead. During the many conversations I'd had while flogging review copies, I'd learnt that book dealers got their best stock by clearing the homes of the recently deceased.

I read and reread the short stories, soaking up the style, the bitter sexuality, hoping for some inspiration. I went to the library and read the obituaries from other newspapers. This was going to be more difficult than I'd first thought. Dahl had been in print well before the *LR*'s first issue. By 1950, when Tony had published a story by him, Dahl already had an agent. His first novel had flopped, but he was well known. Records would exist. A rejected story would have been recycled, sent somewhere else. Dahl was prolific. He was also efficient, a businessman. If he hadn't kept a copy, his agent would have done. Reading about the many tragedies in Dahl's life, I began to think better of exploiting his legacy. Maybe I ought to tell Tony that there was nothing to be found.

Magneta's flat was the top floor of a house in Camden Town, a short tube ride away. I found the house with no difficulty, but the bell was hard to identify. The one I decided upon didn't appear to work. I shouted her and Tim's names several times before my friend appeared at a window. Laughing, he threw down a key.

'Sorry,' he said, as he opened the door on the second floor, 'we're not used to having guests.'

I didn't know what I might find. It was a long time since I'd visited someone's home. Tony, despite his friendliness in the office, had never invited me to his place in Highgate. Magneta, from what little I knew of her, was an old fashioned bohemian. I expected dust, heavy drapes and gothic paraphernalia to match her vivid eye-shadow. Instead I found... normality. There were books on shelves, posters on the walls and two modern art prints, framed. The floorboards had been stripped and varnished, with an Indian rug and a gas fire offering warmth. I couldn't see Magneta, but could smell a rich stew wafting through from the kitchen. The flat reminded me, unbearably, of home, the home that I had left abandoned for more than a year.

'Are you all right?' Tim asked, noticing my mood.

'Fine. Tired, that's all. I've been working hard.'

'Did you bring some of your writing with you?'

'No. I've nothing really ready. Sorry.'

'Never mind. Drink?'

'Please.' Should I have brought a bottle of wine? I wasn't used to domesticity of any kind, wasn't expecting it from Tim. Yet there he was, in clean clothes, neat hair, pouring wine from a box into a proper wine glass. And here was Magneta, hair as wild as before, make-up less so, wearing a loose sweater and woollen leggings.

'I hope you're hungry,' she said. 'It's ready.'

Magneta had made a lentil stew, with celery, mushrooms, carrot, potato and bits of chorizo floating round in it. Before we ate, she dripped olive oil and sherry vinegar over our portions. It was delicious.

'Something I picked up in Spain,' she said, when I praised the dish.

Magneta had lived in Andalusia for a couple of years. It was all tied up with a love affair that went wrong, I gathered, so didn't press her further. Instead I complimented her on the flat.

'We love it. Pity we've got to move out at the end of the year.'

The building, she told me, had been sold months ago. Magneta managed to obtain a cheap, short term lease because she knew the new owner, who was about to restore the place.

'I'll find somewhere else,' she said, 'but not as nice for the price.'

I wondered what she lived on, given that Tim was no longer working, but she got in her answer before my question.

'I suppose I'll have to come up with something pervy to pay the rent. What do you reckon, Tim darling? *I Was A Teenage Love Slave?* Mark, would you like to see my oeuvre?'

She pointed to a shelf that contained half a dozen erotic novels, the sort of thin, tacky paperbacks found on the top shelves of newsagents who didn't normally sell books.

'These are all by you?'

'I'm afraid so.'

The authors were women who sounded as thought they all had big hair. Danielle Colby. Celia Hampton.

'Who makes up the names?'

'The publishers do.'

'Do they take you long to write?'

Magneta looked vaguely insulted. 'Believe it or not, there's a certain amount of talent involved. You have to be able to tell a story, get inside the head of the sort of people who read these things... and write good sex, of course.'

'Who reads them?' I wanted to know. 'Housewives?'

'Theoretically. The publishers did some audience research showing that almost as many men read them as women.'

At random, I opened *Love on the Line*. The opening chapter was a description of a woman rubbing up against a man on the underground. He isn't sure if it's deliberate. Then she reaches inside his raincoat and unzips his fly.

'Take one if you want,' Magneta interrupted my reading.

'No thanks.' I didn't want to read anything that reminded me of my lack of a sex life. But I was beginning to get an inkling of an idea for a short story.

Magneta told me how she'd got into writing the novels through a friend of Tony's.

'When I'm doing my own writing, a three thousand word short story takes me forever. A novel seems like an impossible dream. But with this crap I manage forty thousand words in 'a month. A fortnight, if I really need to.'

'Think you could do it?' Tim asked me.

I shook my head. Maybe I could write formula fiction, if I had to, but I doubted I could write about sex convincingly. In the Greene forgery, I'd been careful not to describe the narrator's sessions with the prostitute.

'You?' I asked Tim.

'I'd try anything, as long as it involved writing. I may have to, soon. We need another place and rents are going through the roof.'

'We don't have to live in London,' Magneta said. 'It might be better for both of us to live somewhere quieter, cheaper for a while.'

'I don't fancy an unheated stone cottage in Andalusia in winter,' Tim said. 'That was Magneta's last suggestion.'

'How about an end terrace in Lancashire?' I said.

'Why do you say that?' Magneta asked.

I explained how I came to have a small house going to waste in Leam. I said that, if the two of them looked after the place and took care of the bills while they were there, then they could have the house for as long as they wanted.

Magneta was enthusiastic. Tim was unsure. 'You're being too generous, Mark. You're a student. We'd be exploiting you.'

'The house has been empty since the September before last,' I pointed out.

Tim and Magneta discussed whether being out of London would hurt their literary careers, coming to the conclusion that neither of them had enough of a career for it to make any difference. Then Magneta asked what I was doing for Christmas.

'Not much,' I said, remembering the previous, bleak Christmas I'd spent alone in a student house.

'Then why don't we spend it together, in your house? You

109

can show us what we need to know about the house and the area. If we all agree that it's a good idea when we're sober, then we'll get everything sorted out then.'

This decided, we celebrated with another drink. My opinion of Magneta had changed totally. She was my new, second-best friend. At the door, she gave me a sloppy kiss.

'Where exactly is Lancashire?' she asked.

I walked home, drunk on wine and friendship. When I got back to my tiny, cold flat above the office, I kept my coat buttoned up, switched on my computer and the single bar electric fire and, more confident than I'd ever been before, began to bash out a story.

Twenty-four

It had come to me as I was looking at Magneta's erotic novel. Why would Roald Dahl write a story for the *Little Review*, then put it aside after Tony's rejection? It had to be because he thought better of it. Not because he'd written a bad story, but because there was something suspect about it, something the world wasn't ready for. 1950 was long before the Lady Chatterley trial. An author couldn't use the 'f' word. Overtly sexual material was beyond the pale.

I might not have the experience to write about sex, but I could imagine a story about somebody writing sex under a pseudonym, like Magneta. Dahl would have written the story, sent it off to Tony, then, when it was rejected, thought better of publishing it. The story could anticipate the sour, sexual subject matter of the *Switch Bitch* stories, written in late middle age. The 1950 Dahl would have worried that readers would think he was writing about himself. By late middle age, if Tony was anything to go by, Dahl wouldn't give a damn.

Dahl didn't have a particularly idiosyncratic style. He sometimes talked to the reader at the beginning of a story, setting the piece up. That was the hardest note to achieve, but it wasn't an essential element. When writing as Dahl, I could rush on with the plot. There was no need for detailed description, but my period in Paris came in useful for the setting. Characterisation wasn't crucial. Narrative was everything. I worked in my knowledge of Jack Kahane's Obelisk, who published *To Beg, I Am Ashamed* and the racy Cecil Barr novels. Dahl might well have read one of Barr's novels, made something of it in his fiction.

When I read the pages back, there was a problem. They didn't sound like Dahl, not for a minute. How could I, who had convincingly forged Hemingway and Greene, have trouble imitating a much lesser author? Even the weakest writer must have a signature style. I wasn't trying to parody Dahl, drawing attention to his weakest elements. And there was more. Although he was educated in England, Dahl wasn't English. Both of his parents were Norwegian. He was an inside outsider, capable of viewing the vagaries of British character with a cold, often cruel eye, which made his voice harder to capture than that of Hemingway or Greene.

There was one possible way around the problem. I could imitate Dahl's first person style. I often found the single viewpoint to be a weakness in first person novels, limiting the action and removing opportunities for suspense. The reader can easily tire of the same voice, finding it monotonous, hectoring, unwelcoming, even smug. But Dahl used it often, so I decided to give this voice a try, pretending to be a Norwegian writing in English. I found a copy of Dahl's first collection, *Someone Like You*. This had several stories written in the first person. They were written in the right period, too. These early stories seemed to have more energy about them than the later work. I began again, starting the story in the middle, rather than at the beginning, and my words began to ring true.

My character introduces himself as Edward Timms, a war veteran with a minor shrapnel injury that causes him to limp. He is wealthy, though at first the source of his wealth isn't clear. Friends assume his money is inherited. Timms has written two novels. They earned him the respect of his peers but didn't sell in great quantities. Timms tells the reader about Lawrence Hamden. Hamden is the author of the *French Maid* series of erotic novels. Many of Timms' friends secretly enjoy his work. Now and then one of those friends asks Edwards what he thinks of Hamden. Edward pretends not to have read him.

By now, most readers will have guessed the secret that my narrator is about to reveal. Timms is not independently wealthy. His money comes from writing erotica under the pseudonym Lawrence Hamden. His publisher, Maurice Cranstone, is a middle-aged Mancunian, partially modelled on Jack Kahane. I described the Hamden stories without having read any erotica of the period, but with a working knowledge of the British bedroom farce, which I felt sure Dahl would be familiar with. As I told it, the Hamden novels were awash with mistaken identity, lust crazed lovers, ridiculous impersonations, the sudden return of spouses and adulterers hiding in unlikely places. The running joke of the series was the sexual sophistication of the French as compared to the English. Men were grateful for the smallest favours of the French maid. On occasion, Hamden's English heroes rescued her from the clutches of the shady con men (usually French) she kept falling for. They were handsomely rewarded, in kind.

Timms finds writing erotica much easier than he does the literary fiction he publishes under his own name. As Hamden's success builds, the impulse to write more serious fiction deserts Timms. Cranstone suggests that he take on a second nom de plume. Timms comes up with Veronica Bendix (using the first and last names of two movie stars of the era). Under that name, he writes a series of 'memoirs' about an amoral female spy in the war just finished. The Bendix books become an even bigger success than the Hamden ones. Veronica Bendix, indeed, becomes the talk of London. Everybody in society wants to know who she is.

At this point of the story I got stuck. I knew that I had to deal with Edward Timms' love life. What sort of relationships did a man who wrote erotic fiction have? If Magneta was anything to go by, perfectly normal ones. I had given Edward a bum leg, like Jake in Hemingway's *The Sun Also Rises*. So he might have trouble finding a girlfriend. Or women might find his injury romantic. I could hint that he was impotent. That would get me out of having to describe his sexual conquests.

I was out of my depth. I kept writing, hoping a solution would present itself. I wrote a cameo appearance for Maurice Cranstone, using what little I knew of Jack Kahane, throwing in a few of Tony's characteristics. But I didn't have a plot, only a situation. I created a woman, Valerie, whom the writer wanted to impress. I based her on Helen Mercer. Valerie was a manipulative, frigid bitch like many women in Dahl's work. She ignored Edward at first, but, as he became wealthier and wealthier, began to attend his flash parties, even accepted his lavish gifts. Still, despite his entreaties, she would not sleep with him.

One night I had the writer, frustrated to the end of his wits, break into her house. He means to seduce her, or, if that fails, to take her by force. When he gets to her bedroom, however, he finds the object of his desire naked, only partially covered by sheets. I hinted that, with one hand out of sight, Valerie was playing with herself.

Yes, that was the taboo twist I needed: masturbation. Even now, decades after *Portnoy's Complaint*, many writers wouldn't discuss it. In 1950, it would have offended most readers. Also, masturbation was the only kind of sex I had any experience of, and could write about convincingly. Would Dahl have written something so explicit? Why not? He liked to shock. No mainstream magazine would have taken the story. Hence he sent it to the *Little Review*, a small subscription literary journal that published risk-taking fiction.

I wrote furiously, ignoring my dry throat and the late hour. Edward interrupts Valerie. He begins a forceful speech. If she will not submit to him, he will have no choice but to take her by force. Then he sees what she's reading and stumbles over

114

his words. It's one of Veronica Bendix's 'memoirs'. He blurts out his authorship, proving his tale by telling her what happens next. Valerie, to his surprise, is not shocked. She tells Edward that if he's half as good a lover as the men he writes about, she'll give him a try.

What would my character do in such circumstances? Run, or risk the humiliation of sexual failure? How would Dahl end the story? I would decide tomorrow. As dawn broke over Soho, I drank a pint of water, which made me feel drunk again, and went to bed. Later, I would have to work out how to forge a convincing manuscript.

The next day was a Friday. After my exertions of the night before, I didn't get up until Tony had left the office. He never came back after lunch on a Friday. He'd left his newspaper open at the obituaries page. At the bottom right, in small print, were the details of Roald Dahl's funeral. I noticed that it was to take place the next day, in Great Missenden, the village where Dahl lived. Which meant, in all likelihood, that his house would be empty.

I was thinking like a burglar. The house would be locked, doubtless well secured. But what about the hut, where, according to the obituary, Dahl did all his writing, sitting in an old armchair? How secure could a hut be? According to the obituary, Dahl wrote his first drafts in pencil on yellow foolscap. Even so, he must type them up afterwards. His typewriter, in all likelihood, would still be there. I would never have a better chance to convincingly forge a Roald Dahl story.

Twenty-five

The train from Marylebone was late, allowing me little room for error. On the forty minute journey, I thought of all sorts of problems that might interfere with my plan. Even supposing I got into the writing hut, and the typewriter was still there, it would take me a good hour and a half to type out the four thousand word story. My best typing speed was fifty words a minute. I had to get used to an old typewriter and avoid making mistakes. Also, I had barely enough old paper to type the story onto. If I botched a couple of pages and had to start over, I might run out.

The easiest solution would be to steal the typewriter. But there were problems with that. I might get caught, which would make me a common criminal. There'd be publicity, which could destroy my future and reflect badly on the *Little Review*. Even if I wasn't caught, the typewriter's theft would alert Dahl's executors to the possibility of forgery. I'd never get away with placing my story in the *LR*. If I was caught typing in the hut, however, what could anyone do? I'd be taken for a nutter, pretending to be Dahl, my childhood hero. I wasn't stealing anything. I'd be an embarrassment, spoiling the day of the funeral. But nobody would want to get the police involved. The family would throw me out on my ear, no doubt, and they would have every right to.

The Aylesbury train took me all the way to Great Missenden, I hurried down the High Street then along the lane that led to Gypsy House. It stood alone in five acres of land on the far side of the train line. The funeral was about to start. Surely there'd be no-one home. I walked around the house's perimeter, looking for a way in.

A thick hedge surrounded the back garden. I peered

through it, trying to make out the hut. When I failed I wasn't sure what to do. I had to allow for the risk of being spotted by servants, or guard dogs. It would be suspicious for me to walk around the boundary again. I wore a heavy denim jacket and jeans. My paper was in a sturdy folder. I zipped it inside my jacket and looked down the lane. Nobody in sight. I tucked my bare hands into the sleeves of my jacket and charged into the hedge.

It hurt far more than I'd expected. Worse, I almost got stuck in the middle. My left knee banged against solid branch. Sharp twigs scratched my face. I half twisted my right ankle as I crashed through the other side, falling onto wet grass where I landed awkwardly on my rump. Slowly, I stood up. At least no guard dog had launched itself at me. I ached all over. My face was bleeding. Bits of hedge stuck to me. But I was through. And there, at the edge of an orchard, was the brick hut, with its white walls and yellow door.

The door opened on the left. There was no key in the lock. I might be able to kick it in, but I wasn't a vandal, and, anyway, to do so would make my presence obvious. I tried the handle, expecting to find the door firmly locked. It wasn't. I pushed open the door.

The hut was dark. There was a small entrance area, then another shadowy doorway. To my right, there were filing cabinets. The large window was covered by a plastic sheet encrusted with grime. There was barely enough light for me to see clearly. On my left, there was a wing-backed armchair with a green felt writing board leaning on it. To the left of that was a small table with an old-fashioned angle poise type lamp, an ashtray and a fairly modern phone. Where was the typewriter? I turned on the lamp. There was no room for a typewriter on the desk to the right of the armchair. This was covered with objects including model aeroplanes, fossils, a cup containing several Dixon Ticonderoga pencils, a little ball of silver foil, a ceramic beetle, a round stone, antique knives and a sword. There were pictures everywhere, but no typewriter.

I stood in the gloom, taking in the atmosphere of the space where a real writer had worked. All his money, yet he had chosen to work in a hut, without basic comforts. I should be able to learn from that.

I was about to go when I saw it. There, on top of one of the black filing cabinets, was an old canvas cover. I reached up. Beneath the cover was a typewriter. I lifted it onto the table by Dahl's armchair, making room by moving the phone. I removed the cover and switched on the lamp, then squatted awkwardly in order to type. I tested my luck with a new sheet of paper. *The quick brown fox jumped over the lazy dog.* I typed this a handful of times until my fingers were sure of the keys. Then I put the piece of paper aside. If I were to be caught, this was the sheet I wanted my captors to see. Now I placed a sheet of 1950's paper from the *LR* archive under the roller. I had memorised the layout Dahl used, and was careful to reproduce it. There were no common errors for me to imitate, as there had been with Hemingway. All I had to aim for was accuracy.

It was cold for early December. But that didn't matter. As I typed, scrunched up awkwardly, barely visible through the large window, I picked up speed and became confident of my chances. I made small embellishments to my original. After a while I began to add new sentences and dialogue. It was as if Dahl was there, in me.

I lost all sense of time. While I was, in a sense, copy typing, I was also thinking ahead. The ending I'd come up with the day before wasn't good enough. What I'd written in Soho didn't feel like Dahl. Masturbation was too tacky a denouement and the twist wasn't clever enough. Still I typed, improving as I went, while a newly discovered part of my brain schemed. As I got to the middle of the story, something happened. A woman appears at the club, accompanied by Timms' friend, Barker. The new character I wrote was still based on Helen, but a decade or so older and only moderately vampish. Timms is immediately taken with her, and wonders how Barker has snagged her. Then his friend introduces the pair. Her name, he says, is Veronica Bendix.

I had my twist. Timms can't call the woman's bluff without revealing that he himself is Bendix. Anyway, he's intrigued as to why this woman, an adventurer if ever there was one, is pretending to be his pseudonym. He wants to be with her. So he contrives to get rid of Barker and invites 'Veronica' to dinner. She agrees enthusiastically.

The next night, they meet. 'Veronica', it transpires, is a great fan of Edward's literary work, dismissing her 'own' novels as insignificant twaddle. Timms quizzes her about whether her wartime memoirs have any basis in reality. She asks him whether it would bother him if they weren't true. He admits that it would bother him more if they were.

They would be back from the funeral by now, I was sure. But what reason would anyone have to come to this shed? I had to keep writing. I had to find out what happened next. As I continued to type, developing a romance in which both parties were lying to the other, I began to get an inkling of how the story should end. 'Veronica' and Edward become lovers. I wrote a scene where Timms goes to see his publisher, Cranstone, to deliver the latest French maid book, and tells him that he is unable to write any more of the Bendix spy memoirs. Cranstone says he's mad. The Bendix books are out-selling his others by ten to one and, with the relaxation of censorship imminent in the UK, sales could go through the roof. But Timms is adamant.

When he proposes to Veronica, she is unable to consider his offer she says, until he knows the truth. She admits that she is not really Veronica Bendix, that she took on that identity as a lark for his friend, but fell for Edward and couldn't work out how to escape the situation. He replies that it's all right, he knew all along that she was lying, because...

There was a noise from the far end of the garden, but it was too late to stop now. I knew how my story must end. Dahl was dictating the story to me through his typewriter. I was merely his amanuensis, tapping out the words with scarcely a mistake. Veronica agrees to marry Timms, but on one condition, that he resume writing the novels that had drawn her to him in the first place. But what would they live on, he asks. You're forgetting, she tells him, that you're marrying the best selling writer, Veronica Bendix. Your friends will envy you and, with your help, I can become the writer we both pretended to be.

Was this too rosy an ending? I could think of another twist or two, but too many twists might prevent the story resonating with the reader. Anyway, only one blank sheet of paper remained. I typed a title page: *The Woman Who Married Herself by Roald Dahl*, in the same format as the story Dahl submitted to the *Little Review*. Once I finished typing, I could hear movement outside. I checked my watch. I'd been in the shed for more than two hours.

I was replacing the typewriter when I saw a young face outside the dirty window. Too late, I turned off the light. The lad was running to the house. What had he seen? I must look like a scarecrow, for I was still covered in bits from the hedge. As I shoved the papers into my folder I could hear the boy screaming. I opened the door. No-one was in sight.

I was girding myself to jump back through the hedge when I heard rapid footsteps. At least two sets, possibly three. If I jumped through the hedge, I'd be heard. The only place to hide was behind the shed.

'I'm telling you,' a child's voice said, 'I saw Grandpa's ghost!'

'Now, now, you're imagining things,' a woman's voice told him. 'Grandpa's gone to heaven.'

'Grandpa didn't believe in heaven. He told me. I know it was him. I heard the typewriter. He had his light on.'

'It's not on now. Doesn't look as though anybody's been in here. The window's so filthy I'm surprised you could see a thing.'

'I'm telling you, I saw Grandpa, only he didn't look old. He had hair, but there were twigs and things in it, like he'd dug his way out of the ground.'

'That isn't funny. It sounds to me, young man, as if you've inherited your grandfather's bizarre sense of humour. Now, he can't have dug his way out of the ground, because we buried him not half an hour ago. Get back to the house and play with your cousins if you know what's good for you!'

'But I saw him, I saw him...' The boy's voice faded as he hurried away. I thought that I was safe. But the man hadn't gone. Anxious to escape, I nearly walked into him. Luckily, he had his back to me. He spoke to the woman. She was rather beautiful, and this made me all the more guilty for my intrusion.

'Let's take a look,' he said.

The door was opened. Still I didn't dare move. I pressed my ear against the wall of the shed as they moved about.

'See that muck on the floor? I swept it clean before.'

'We probably walked it in ourselves just now.'

'Is there a typewriter in here?'

'I don't think so.'

There was a silence, followed by the man again.

'Feel this lamp. It's warm!'

A longer pause.

'It doesn't matter. Nothing's been taken.'

'But... what happened?'

'Nothing happened. Let's go.'

Once I'd heard the door being locked behind them I counted to a hundred then got out of the garden the way I'd got in. Shaking off twigs and dirt, I walked back to the station.

I didn't dare check the manuscript on the journey home. I thought through the plot I'd created, looking for holes, and couldn't find any. Once I got back to the empty *LR* office, I read the typescript carefully. The title gave a little of the plot away, but I was stuck with it. I wouldn't get near Dahl's typewriter again. The typewriter might not be the same as the one used for the earlier story. I couldn't be sure about this, but it didn't matter. I'd used Dahl's typewriter, after all. Elated by my achievement, I took the ancient paper clip from the old story and put it on the new one, which I then inserted into a manila envelope from the files marked '1951: miscellaneous'. I hoped my forgery would acquire an early 1950's aroma by Monday, when I would show it to Tony.

Twenty-six

Tony didn't come into the office on Monday morning. This sometimes happened when he'd had a big weekend. I wasn't sure what his 'big weekend's involved, but could always tell when he'd had one by the bags beneath his eyes. On a good day, Tony could pass for his late fifties. On a bad day, he looked every one of his sixty-seven years. There was the usual huge pile of manuscripts, Saturdays being when most part-time scribblers felt the need to unburden their souls in brown, heavy duty, A5 envelopes. I took my time sorting through them. Amidst the usual rubbish I found that Tim had sent a story, *New Moon*, about four strangers who spend the night in a strange hotel where the staff all disappear. It was too soon to send a story, in the sense that Tim had a piece in the current issue. Yet, given his five year wait for that to appear, it was high time to consider him again.

I read the story at once. Tim's style had developed, changed. Did it work? I couldn't tell. I was friendly with its author. How could I separate the words on the page from the person I knew? I wanted to like the story because I was spending Christmas with Tim. So I liked it a lot. But I had no idea what Tony would think.

Lunchtime was long over and Tony still hadn't shown up, so, for the first time in the year I'd been at the magazine, I rang him at home. He was ex-directory, otherwise he would have been bothered by contributors, but had given me the number 'for emergencies'. Was this an emergency? There was nobody, to my knowledge, who would notice if Tony had been taken ill. The phone rang and rang, which was odd, because I knew he had an answering machine. It was probably nothing, but I was getting worried. I left it an hour, then located his address in an A to Z and took a tube to Highgate.

Tony lived in a ground floor flat. What would I do if, when I got there, nobody answered the door? Call a neighbour, or the police? I didn't know. The street he lived on was less expensive looking than I'd imagined. His house was one of the more dilapidated ones. The windows were dirty. It was a dingy day and the windows had net curtains, not something I'd have associated with Tony. It was impossible to see anything going on inside. I rang the bell and waited. No reply. I rang again. Still nothing. I wondered whether his neighbours worked. I'd never heard Tony mention either of them. Which bell should I ring next: the top or ground floor? I was about to press the lower one when a voice hissed over the intercom.

'Who's there?'

'Tony? It's me, Mark. You didn't answer your phone, so...'

A buzzer sounded and I pushed the front door open. In the dark hall, mail was piled on top of a doorless cupboard that housed three electricity meters. There were several letters for Tony. I picked them up. What was wrong with him if he couldn't even make it to the front door?

The door to his flat badly needed painting. I knocked lightly and it opened.

'I'm sorry you had to drag yourself out here.'

Tony was wearing a red, silk dressing gown. I stepped onto thick pile carpet. His flat had crimson painted walls festooned with an odd mishmash of paintings. But it was Tony who claimed my attention. His left eye had been blackened and his jaw was swollen. A recent spurt of blood stained his upper lip.

'Have you seen a doctor?' I asked. 'Been to Casualty?'

Tony shook his head. 'Too humiliating.'

'You don't have to say how it happened.'

'Dear boy, they take one look at me and they know.'

'My mum taught me first aid. Let me take a proper look, clean you up.'

'There's no need...' Tony murmured.

'It's either that or I call a taxi this minute and get you to Casualty.'

'Very well. But...'

'No buts. Where's your medicine cupboard?'

As I located iodine, TCP, Savlon, cotton wool and sticking plasters, I felt myself going into role. The calming voice I used with Tony was my mother's, the one she used with me when I'd been beaten up by bullies.

'Did he take much?' I asked, as I finished cleaning his cuts and bruises.

'Money. A radio. A few CDs. Nothing really valuable.'

Tony was naked beneath his gown. He'd put cream on the bruises he could reach. I applied more, turning a blind eye to the way his wrinkled penis hardened as I rubbed the Deep Heat lotion into his bruised thighs. After making a cup of tea and getting him to go back to bed, I gave him the good news.

'I found the Dahl story you didn't use.'

'You did?' Tony managed a strange smile. 'That's very good.'

'Having read it, I think I know why Dahl never published it.'

'Never published it, you say? That's a stroke of luck. Why would that be?'

'Too clever-clever for its time, almost post modern. Read it for yourself when you're back in the office. I wouldn't want to spoil it for you.'

For the first time, Tony smiled properly, revealing that his attacker had knocked out one of his front teeth. 'Who's to say that I don't remember it from all those years ago?'

I told him the title. 'Ring any bells?'

Tony shook his head. 'Mark, I don't know what I'd do without you.'

Before I left, when he was himself again, Tony told me. 'Take the rest of the month off. I intend to. I need a holiday, somewhere hot.'

'I'm going away for Christmas. But until then, I'll mind the office. What do you want me to do with submissions?'

'Send them all back, tell them we're full up until 1999, I don't care. Unless they're from people we've asked to be in the five hundredth issue.'

'OK.' I was disappointed that he wasn't rushing to read my Dahl story.

'Thanks for coming here,' Tony said, 'for helping. I owe...'

'Nonsense,' I told him. 'You'd do the same for me.'

Tony nodded. 'We've neither of us got anybody,' he started to say, in the voice he used when he was being wise, paternal. But then he burst into tears, spoiling the effect. I felt awkward. After handing him a tissue, I made my escape.

Back at the office, I was in sole charge of the *Little Review*. I sent Tim a card acknowledging his story and explaining that it would be a while before he heard. Then I rejected the rest of the pile with the appropriate lie. There were two weeks to go before Christmas and I had nothing much to do. I returned to my room and did the only thing I knew how to do. I wrote.

Pretending, as usual, to be somebody else.

Twenty-seven

Magneta bought an ancient but roadworthy Morris Traveller, into which we loaded all of her and Tim's stuff. There was no room left for Tim and me, so we travelled by train, arriving in Leam two days before Christmas. This was, Tim confided in me, the first Christmas that he'd not spent with his family in Reading.

'I've never even been to Lancashire before,' he said, as though there were something romantic about the county. We walked away from the station into a cold wind, pressing on through street after street of grey stone terraced houses and small shops festooned with Christmas decorations. I pointed out the library where my mother used to work. Tim asked me about her. I told him the barest details.

'What about your father?' Tim asked.

'I never knew him.'

'But who was he?'

I gave the old answer. 'A fellow student, I think. I don't know if he buggered off or my mum decided not to tell him she was pregnant by him. Either way, he was never mentioned.'

Sensing my discomfort, Tim changed the subject. 'Everywhere you look, it's like stepping back into the fifties. What a great place to write!'

It was true. After fifteen months in London, returning to Leam was like going through a time warp.

'This is it,' I told Tim, as we turned into the semicircle of alms cottages. Curtains twitched as I fumbled the key to the front door. I wondered how many of our neighbours had died since I was last here. As a child, I'd got used to death. Every winter took one or two of our neighbours away. My mother couldn't hide where they'd gone.

At the front door, Mum's death assaulted me afresh. For a moment, as I stepped inside, I could smell her, sense her, as if she still occupied this dark, dingy house. But then I switched on a light and Tim commented on the mildew. I hurried to the gas fire, promising that we'd get the walls dried out before Magneta arrived in the car.

'This place is terrific!' Tim announced, a wild grin spreading across his face. 'It's just right for us.'

I went upstairs and dumped my stuff in my old bedroom. The mattress on my single bed felt damp. I fetched an old electric blanket from the attic. Back downstairs, Tim had the kettle on. There was a pile of mail two feet high for me to sort through. The only letter I opened was from Mr Darkland, the solicitor. He informed me of the legal ramifications of my letting the house to friends and suggested I give them a short term assured six month renewable tenancy at a peppercorn rent, so that there could be no issue of their getting squatters' rights. I put the letter aside, intending to ignore it.

Tim poured tea and began to enthuse about all the writing he meant to get done. My room, once I'd returned to London, would become his study. Magneta would use the living room.

'Or the other way round, if she prefers.'

By the time Magneta arrived, the house was, at least, warm, though much of the heat fled as we unloaded her and Tim's possessions from the car. Magneta immediately professed herself in love with the place and amazed that I hadn't returned before.

'It's not home since Mum died. It's just the place where I grew up.'

'Have you got a lot of friends to catch up with?' she asked.

'I've not stayed in touch with anyone.'

Since leaving school, over two years before, I hadn't seen any of the handful of people I used to hang out with. The only friends I'd made in London were Tony, Tim and Magneta. They seemed to sense this, for Magneta didn't pursue the subject. Instead, the three of us planned Christmas. There were ten days before I had to be in London to sign on again, though I wasn't sure whether I should stay that long. While I read some of the mail, Tim and Magneta went shopping.

Soon, ten days seemed too short. We slept late, ate big meals, drank, smoked dope, listened to music and watched television. Seeing Tim and Magneta together, I began to understand something of how intimacy between a man and a woman worked. At first I worried, because they either bickered and teased each other or hardly seemed to talk to the other at all (though both would talk at length with me.) At times, Magneta seemed to dominate Tim. But I couldn't help hearing them in bed, at night. The Magneta I heard in the next room sounded vulnerable, in love, nothing like the dominatrix I'd imagined.

That Christmas, Magneta's looks were changing. She'd stopped dying her hair. Her roots, as they appeared, were a gingery brown. Without the gothic make-up, she looked younger. Magneta was, Tim told me when I finally found a tactful way to ask the question, twenty-nine, only two and a half years older than him. That the couple didn't have long conversations when I was around, I slowly realised, was out of politeness, and because they didn't need to. They had absolute faith in each other. They chose not to draw attention to their self sufficiency because to do so would only serve to emphasise my loneliness.

Magneta and Tim quickly made friends with the old folks who surrounded us. Magneta proudly told them that Tim was a proper writer, while she wrote dirty books to support him. The neighbours loved this. Magneta had a far more impressive track record than Tim, but she played it down.

New Year came and went and it was time for me to return to London, to my cold flat above the *LR* office, to nine more months before I began my University studies again. I would have preferred to stay in Leam. But Tim and Magneta were ready to begin their new life together and I needed to start over.

'We insist on paying you some rent,' Tim said, as they drove me to the station. 'No argument or we won't stay.'

I acquiesced. 'Whatever you can afford.'

Both hugged me goodbye.

'Come back and visit any time,' Magneta said, and I promised that I would.

Soho was windy and icy, so much so that it was almost denuded of tourists. The office was as I'd left it. Tony, it seemed, was still on holiday. There was a week before term started, and I could — if I chose — attend the lectures I'd skipped the previous year. After my Christmas with Tim and Magneta, I felt more rounded, as though I were ready for anything.

Twenty-eight

The *LR's* mail basket was overflowing. Many letters were postmarked the 27th, suggesting that the sender had used the holiday to prepare a submission for the *Little Review*. Amidst the pile of manuscripts submitted were two Christmas cards for me. One was from Francine, with an affectionate message. The other was postmarked New York, where I knew only two people. *Hope to see you in the New Year* it said, with no mention of the money from the Hemingway manuscripts. The card was signed Helen and Paul Mercer.

I was forging again, but in a purer way. I was writing for my own satisfaction, adopting the style of James Sherwin because, as yet, I had no style of my own. Few authors, Tony reckoned, found their own voice before thirty. The same went for their subject matter. I could find nothing of my own to write about, so borrowed Sherwin's subject, as well as his style. I was simulating the Sherwin novel he'd never published, the one he was reading extracts from when my mother saw him read on a university tour in the early seventies. *A Commune* was the working title.

James Sherwin was like JD Salinger, Harper Lee and Ralph Ellison, all of whom had had huge early success then lapsed into silence. Each writer's first novel had continued to sell, so they had no need to keep publishing new books to make a living. Rather than dilute his or her reputation, the author stopped publishing. What I wanted to know was this: did Sherwin stop writing, too? Rumour had it that Salinger and Ellison still wrote every day. Salinger was supposed to keep his manuscripts in a safe the size of a room. Ellison was said to be working on his second novel, and — decades ago — had published chapters from the work-in-progress. When each died, this hidden writing was likely to be published quickly. Sherwin was younger than those two and had been less popular. But he was the most successful recluse. He lived cheaply on a remote Greek island with an irregular ferry service and a much younger American wife. He didn't want to be disturbed and I wouldn't disturb him, no matter how strong my obsession.

As my Sherwin voice grew more convincing, there was a temptation to test it on somebody. But it was a temptation I resisted. James Sherwin's 1960's stories (including the two in the *LR*) had all been collected. There were so few of them, he was unlikely to have forgotten one. There was no way I could convincingly discover a short story that Sherwin was meant to have written thirty years before. Anyway, if the Dahl story came out, I couldn't get away with the *we found it in the archives* line again. My Sherwin stuff was an exercise, much as I'd intended the Hemingway forgeries to be. It was destined for the bottom drawer.

On January 4th, I collected the mail from the large wire basket at the bottom of the mail chute. Amidst the brown A5 envelopes was a postcard from Tunisia, announcing that Tony was having such a good time he had extended his holiday (no word of his return date), a review copy of a small press poetry book (it had to be small press because no proper publisher would be back at work for another week yet) and a blue, airmail envelope, postmarked Greece.

I put the latter in Tony's personal pile and worked my way through the day's submissions. Rejecting the lot took the best part of an hour. I wondered how the would-be contributors would feel if they knew that their work had been tossed aside after a cursory glance from a nineteen year old university dropout. Then I picked up the blue envelope again. Who would be writing to Tony from Greece? It wasn't a contribution. I could tell from the weight of the envelope that it held only one sheet of paper. There was no necessity to open it.

James Sherwin lived in Greece. And Tony had told me to acknowledge any contributions we received for the five hundredth issue. This letter might be a contribution, I told myself, a short poem on a single sheet of paper. Before I could think of an objection to this argument, I opened the envelope. Inside was a word processed letter.

Karenos, December 14th, 1990

Dear Tony,

Thanks for your letter and the book. Five hundred! You have my heartiest congratulations. Do send me a copy of the anniversary issue. It's been a long while, hasn't it? This is the worst time of year on the island, cold, windy, nearly deserted, almost makes me yearn for London. I think I wrote to tell you that I married. Sonia bought me this computer in the hope that it would get me writing again, but all I seem to write on it are replies to prissy American doctoral students telling them to fuck off. Most days though, I sit down at the damned machine, try.

Which is my way of saying that I haven't anything to offer you just now, but if something crops up, I'll send it your way. I enjoyed the poems, particularly 'His Trojan Ass'. Good to know that somebody's as lusty as ever.

warm regards,
James

The letter surprised me. For a start, I hadn't known Sherwin and Tony were pally. That somebody of Sherwin's stature liked Tony's poems made me want to read them myself. I'd glanced at them, but hadn't been to one of Tony's (now very occasional) readings. From his letter, Sherwin — whom I thought of as an almost mythical, godlike figure — appeared very human, a man with a simple case of writer's block that had lasted twenty years.

I felt guilty about reading the letter. It was intended for Tony, not for me. But I also felt excited, not by the content, but by the medium. I could tell at a glance that James Sherwin owned exactly the same computer and printer as I did: an Amstrad 8256 with a bog standard dot matrix printer. Nobody could possibly distinguish one machine's printout from the other. A forger's delight. But the excitement soon passed, for the coincidence had no consequences. There was nothing I could do to profit from this discovery, nothing at all.

As the days rolled by, more contributions came in for the five hundredth issue. The Arts Board had yet to inform us about the grant, but they could hardly withdraw it before the anniversary issue. And there was no word from Tony.

Then, one day in the middle of the month, he was back. Hearing movement in the office below me, I hurried downstairs, shivering, wearing only my underpants. It was eight, very early for Tony. He hobbled up the stairs, tanned but tired. It was the first time I'd seen him use a walking stick. He thanked me for holding the fort.

'That attack shook me badly. I didn't know how much until I got away. But I've been gone far too long. You must tell me everything.'

I told him as much as I thought he could take in, finishing with the letter from Sherwin, which he examined almost lovingly.

'I haven't heard from James in years.'

'You used to be friends?'

Tony nodded his head, not looking at me. Were they more than friends? But no, Sherwin couldn't be gay. He had recently married.

'I'll take this pile to read at home,' Tony told me. 'I'm going to put together a contents list for the five hundredth issue to show to the Arts Board. That and the sales increase should guarantee our grant for the next couple of years.'

'I hope so,' I said, then added. 'Oh, I put a story by Tim Cooper in the pile. I thought you might want at least one new writer in the anniversary issue.'

'Good idea,' Tony said, adding, after a while, 'you haven't written anything you want me to look at, have you?'

'I'm not ready yet,' I told him.

'Not necessarily for publication,' Tony said, in his mildest voice. 'But it can help to have an audience, especially when you're starting out. You can leap frog some of the more obvious pitfalls, not get into bad habits, that kind of thing.'

'I see,' I said, noncommittally.

'I really would like to help,' Tony told me, kindly. 'You've helped me so much.'

'I am writing,' I explained, awkwardly. 'Only, most of it sounds like whatever writer I've just been reading.'

'Everybody starts with imitation,' Tony told me. 'It's inevitable. I started out trying to sound exactly like Auden. Early Auden. These days, I keep reminding myself of late Auden, though no-one else seems to notice. It's OK. It's not something to worry about, believe me.'

If only he knew. 'I'd like a copy of one of your books,' I told Tony. 'the one with the poem that Sherwin mentions, maybe.'

'Sure,' Tony said. 'I'll bring one in tomorrow. And thanks again for all your help, Mark. You've been a brick.'

I left to attend one of the lectures I'd skipped the previous year. The lecturer was even duller than I remembered. As I was leaving, a pretty student who was sitting on the same row as me said 'I've not seen you before. Are you in our year?'

She was chatting me up, not challenging me. Still I didn't know how to react. I mumbled something and hurried away, wondering why I was so useless with women. I didn't go to any more lectures after that.

Twenty-nine

The five hundredth issue was coming together. The artist Francis Bacon, an old chum of Tony's, had agreed to contribute an illustration for the cover. Tony returned from the Colony Club cock-a-hoop with this news. His magnanimity fuelled by champagne, he attributed his good fortune to me.

'Since you've been on board, Mark, things have really turned around.'

'When are you going to publish it?' I asked, unmoved. The issue was already late. Tony had decided that it would be a double number, incorporating issue 501, allowing him to charge a full fiver for a copy.

'As soon as the Arts Board cheque arrives and I can pay the printer's bill. I have a meeting with them next week.'

'And is the Dahl story going in?' Since his return I'd been avoiding asking him about my forgery. I didn't want to cast suspicion on the story or jinx it in any way.

'Ah,' he replied, instantly sobering up. 'Now that's a little complicated.'

'Why?'

'Because Dahl's dead. The thing is, had I accepted the story before his death, that would have been fine. But I rejected it and evidently held onto it for the best part of forty years. I have no right to publish. The question is, do I approach his estate and ask them whether I can use it? In which case, they have every right to say 'no, hand it over'. Or do I publish and be damned, which could get me into trouble?'

None of this had occurred to me. 'Do you think anyone would suppress the story because of its content?' I asked Tony.

'Nah. The sex is at a remove, after all. But a lawyer might argue that Dahl disposed of the story because it wasn't good enough.'

I took a deep breath. 'Do you think it's good enough?'

'I do,' Tony said. 'But it's atypical. What did you think of it?'

I hadn't prepared an answer to that question. I was proud of my work, yet worried that Tony was testing me. He might suspect.

'I'm not a big Dahl fan,' I said. 'But I liked it.'

'Would you publish it in our five hundredth issue?' Tony asked, with one eyebrow raised.

I didn't answer this directly. Instead, I furrowed my brow in thought, then came up with an answer to the question that was most on my mind: how to pass off my forgery convincingly.

'What if you say that Dahl didn't want the story publishing until after he was dead? You accepted it, but then he changed his mind.'

'A little far fetched,' Tony told me, then began to think about it. 'Surely I'd have kept the correspondence?'

'All sorts of things get lost,' I told him. 'And Dahl was a very minor writer then. You'd forgotten all about the story until you read about his death, and then you sent your assistant burrowing in the archives...'

Tony laughed. 'It might work. I never realised you were such an accomplished liar, Mark. I'll think about it. Here.' He held out a slim volume. 'The book you asked for. I hope you enjoy it, but don't tell me if you don't.'

It was *Purposes of Regimentation*, Tony's latest Carcanet collection. Inside it he'd written *For Mark, without whom I cannot do without* which I found a little ambiguous, though I know he meant it in an affectionate way. I smiled gratefully, then returned to my room, where I worked on the Sherwin story.

Later, at night, I looked at the poems. Some I understood, some I didn't. Whether this was a failure on my part or because they were deliberately obscure, I can't say. Tony wasn't an 'out' gay poet, like Thom Gunn, but, if you knew him it was hard not to read a majority of the poems as being about gay sex. They were, in turn, whimsical, erotic and vaguely disappointed. Leaving aside two affecting elegies for friends who had died of AIDS, the poems did little for me. I kept the book upstairs, but, as Tony had suggested, never mentioned it to him again.

This was a lonely time. Tony spent no more than an hour or two in the office each day. Tim was in Leam. We wrote to each other, but he and Magneta hadn't had the phone reconnected. I could make free phone calls from the office, but there was nobody to have a conversation with. I developed ways of filling the hours. Thanks to a letter of accreditation from Tony, I had a reader's ticket for the British Library. At first I felt like an impostor amongst the academics and obsessives who inhabited the grand building. Yes, as I tracked down every published article about James Sherwin, my own minor obsession, I began to feel like one of them.

I found the early poems and a letter he'd had published in *The Times*. There were two uncollected stories in long disappeared magazines from the early 60s. I got a clutch of interviews and countless articles about his work. There were even a number of *whatever happened to?* and *the mystery of* type pieces, though these appeared to have dried up since the mid 80s.

I read and I wrote and I lived on porridge, pasta and sandwiches. I was poor. The dole was pathetic. I could have pulled some kind of scam with housing benefit, perhaps, given that I wasn't paying rent, but I was getting a little rent (which I didn't declare) from Tim and Magneta and that kept me afloat. A prostitute I was on nodding terms with offered me a job putting her cards in telephone boxes. I refused, then regretted my nervous reaction for days. The job would have been good for material.

The nights were long. It was too noisy to get to sleep until late and too cold to walk the streets of Soho, 'researching' material for my novel about London life. I watched my mother's old portable TV, though the reception was bad. I became addicted to American cop shows and *Coronation Street*. I let my hair grow long because I couldn't afford a haircut. All of my clothes were beginning to look shabby. I hadn't bought new ones since Mum's death. I talked to myself a lot. I was, without realising it, rapidly sinking.

As was the magazine. The next Arts Board meeting was cancelled, our grant further delayed. There then followed a long silence. The absent Tony kept getting phone calls from the small printers he'd been using since 1972.

'He owes us nearly four thousand. That's a month's payroll.'

The *Little Review* had been run on a shoe string for years. Nominally, it paid people, but most contributors waived payment. Tony, assuming that his annual grant would be renewed, had been juggling debtors to keep the cash flow going. Doubtless he'd done this a hundred times before. In the early days, he once told me proudly, 'There were no grants, and I made a small profit, out of which I paid myself. In those days, you see, people had a real appetite for literature.'

But those days were long gone. Without a grant, there wasn't a single literary magazine that could survive, unless you counted the small offset jobs that looked like bad photocopies and were produced by angry, unemployed men in northern towns. And maybe they were the only ones that deserved to survive, though I was too tactful to say this to Tony. I'd been brought up to believe in being self sufficient, and hated drawing the dole. Wasn't a grant a kind of dole for magazines? Wouldn't it be better to use the money to pay budding authors forty quid a week on a job creation scheme? I did try that one on Tony.

'Half the scroungers on the streets would claim to be writers,' he objected.

'Then make them produce a hundred pages every three months or they lose their money,' I suggested. 'That'd cure a writer's block.'

'The trouble is,' Tony told me, changing tack, 'what we need are fewer writers, not more. The ones we have can't make a living.'

The printers threatened to take him to court. Tony had nearly gone bankrupt in the late seventies. He was getting too old to be put through that again. He began to pester Naomi Finch, the Arts Board officer responsible for the *Little Review*'s funding. After a week of daily phone calls, Finch invited Tony to a meeting. When he came back, he was lower than I'd seen him before.

'They're pulling the plug,' he told me. 'Magazine support budgets are being slashed and we're the biggest to go. This is what she said to me: *magazines have a time when they're vital — a couple of years, five at the most — after which they become like an aging slag who's slept with everybody but never had the sense to get married and settle down. She's always trying to pull the new talent, not realising that, in satisfying her jaded appetites, she's depriving somebody else of a good fuck.*

'Then she told me formally that the board felt it was time for the *Little Review* to make way for new magazines. What new magazines? I said to her. She couldn't answer, of course. So I started my spiel about the five hundredth issue, all the people who were going to be in it and you know what she said? Why don't you write to them all? See if they'll stump up for the printing bill and go out with a bang? As if I could humiliate myself by...'

He burst into tears and, awkwardly, I hugged him, feeling useless and sorry for my friend. Sorry for myself too, for soon I would be out of a job.

Thirty

Tony began to take the magazine very seriously indeed. He started coming in at ten, opening the mail and answering the phone himself. He wrote to a handful of people: rich bene-factors who had come through in the past and authors who had made it big (fewer than you might think: most successful writers still earned less than school teachers). He needed ten thousand pounds to cover the overdue printing bill and the costs of the final issue. I suggested he go to Francis Bacon, who was, reputedly, a millionaire. His cover sketch alone was worth many times the amount needed. Tony wouldn't hear of it. He wouldn't sell art, and he wouldn't put himself in an embarrassing position with a friend.

'Do you know the hoops I had to jump through to get Francis to volunteer an illustration for the cover without actu-ally asking him for one?'

'Couldn't you mention your problems in the Colony? Surely he'd offer...'

'People aren't naive, Mark. Not nice, either, most of them. I can just hear one or two people's sneering tones should I even bring it up. *Bracken's on his uppers. Watch out, Francis, Tony's after a loan. Didn't you give him a picture already?* I'll get the money somehow, even if I have to sell the lease on this place. Ten grand's not that much.'

'Sell the lease?'

I didn't know that the *Little Review* owned the lease to the building, but the prospect of being homeless sharpened my mind. I asked Tony to explain the situation. It turned out that he owned the lease to the whole building, subletting to the porn shop below, which effectively paid the *LR*'s rent, rates and heating bills.

'The lease runs out in four years. I was planning to pack up then, sell the archive, maybe publish the occasional chapbook of poetry, but basically retire.'

'Couldn't you sell the archive now?' I asked.

'Hardly. These things take months, years even, to negotiate. The archive isn't catalogued to anywhere near the necessary standards. I want the five hundredth issue to come out this year. Anyway, I'm not sure it's worth a great deal. I suppose the unpublished Dahl story would be the icing on the cake for anybody buying it. But that would depend on it being properly authenticated.'

I looked away. The Chinese supermarket down the road was busy today. Four or five customers were queuing to pay. However, the narrow road was at that moment blocked by their vegetable supplier's mini-van. A taxi was sounding its horn. Tony coughed.

'What will you do about the Dahl?' I asked.

'It would be foolish not to try and publish,' Tony told me. So I've decided to get it set in print. I'll send a set of proofs to Dahl's home to cover myself...'

'And if somebody objects?'

'Take legal advice, I suppose.'

'Shouldn't you do that first?' I asked.

Tony gave me a condescending look. 'Legal advice costs,' was all he said.

'But shouldn't we make a profit on the final issue?' I asked, trying to be optimistic. Then I realised what I'd done. The unsayable had slipped out, that the next issue would be the last one ever. My face must have reddened. Tony, seeing my embarrassment, didn't comment on my mistake.

'Theoretically, the last issue made a profit,' he said. 'But it will be months before we know how much money came in. Lots of shops we haven't dealt with before took copies. That isn't to say that they'll pay us for them. The distributors took an extra thousand, but they only pay us forty-seven percent of the cover price. If you don't take our grants into account, we lose money on those sales. By putting up the cover price of the five hundredth issue, I can get around that, but we probably won't sell as many copies.'

He lit a cigarette. 'There isn't much money to be made in this game, Mark. Take my advice. While you're waiting to become a writer, don't start a magazine. It will suck up all the energy you need to make a real career out of writing. Your best years go and you don't even notice because you're too busy, keeping the thing going, giving other writers their break. And what thanks do you get? Bugger all. You're seen as a bloodsucker by the grant giving bodies, who can't wait to get rid of you and reward someone newer. Most writers hate you, because you won't publish them. Or if you do, you take too long, or don't take the next one, and they resent you for building them up, then knocking them down. It's a mug's game.'

'You must have got something out of it,' I said, weakly.

'I never paid myself more than a token amount. I used to get laid a little — not a lot, but enough to make it seem worthwhile. And my own work has always been noticed, quite well reviewed — nobody wants to make an enemy out of a well known editor. Nobody wants to praise you too much, either, in case it looks like toadying. Then there's the satisfaction of the magazine itself, of course. Seeing it in the shops, on people's shelves, perfect bound and shining with promise. But that doesn't compare with the satisfaction of having a real writing career.'

'Why have you kept at it, then?' I asked. 'I mean... forty years.'

'I'd have thought that was obvious,' Tony told me, pouring

himself a glass of Famous Grouse. 'It's the only thing I know how to do.'

He offered me a drink, which I refused.

'There's one good side to all this,' Tony said, as I went upstairs to work. 'At least I'll never have to send out another rejection slip.'

When I went back downstairs it was dark. Tony never worked this late, but there was a light on in the office, so I looked in on my way out for something to eat. Tony was still there, glass of whisky in one hand, cigarette in the other. He wasn't alone. Tony raised his glass and called my name.

'There's somebody I want you to meet.'

There, in the chair that I normally occupied, was a middle-aged man with a red face and an expensive suit. It was Paul Mercer.

Thirty-one

'Mark, this is Paul Mercer. Paul, I'd like you to meet my editorial assistant and archivist, Mark Trace.'

Paul stood up and shook my hand. Should I reveal at once how I used to work for Paul and he'd ripped me off over the Hemingway manuscripts? It would be the open way to behave. Tony would understand why I'd never mentioned it before. But he'd also work out what other manuscripts I'd forged.

By hesitating, I let the moment pass.

'Paul acts as an agent for various American university libraries,' Tony told me. 'He's interested in buying our archive.'

'Really?' I said. Again, Paul had come to steal. This time not from me, but from Tony.

'Tony tells me that most of the stuff is in the flat upstairs,' Paul said in his brash, booming voice.

'I think Paul would like to see it,' said Tony.

'Sure,' I said. 'Now?'

'If you don't mind...'

I didn't mind. This way, I would get Paul on his own, for Tony disliked the climb. I led Paul up the steep stairs to the box room.

'Helen sends her love,' Paul told me, once we were out of earshot. 'She was very keen to know how you're getting on. Next time I come, I'll bring her over. Right now, though, she's real busy with her studies at NYU.'

I didn't take the bait and ask how Helen was or what she was studying. Seeing Paul, overweight and overconfident, thinking of him having her, made me want to vomit.

'Here it is.' I showed him the box room where the magazine's archives were arranged in a semblance of order. For the next half hour, with a librarian's detachment, I ran through some of the highlights of what was there: Albee, Auden, Beckett, Pinter, Plath, Sherwin...

Paul didn't hide his mounting delight.

'I can think of institutions that'll cream their jeans to get their hands on this lot,' he told me, in a rancid, insinuating voice that expected me to share his jubilation. 'I'll take photocopies back to the States with me.'

'We don't have a photocopier,' I said. I wasn't going to let any of this stuff out of the building, not after what had happened to my Hemingway stories.

'A magazine with no copier! How awfully British!'

'You owe me some money,' I told him, annoyed by his attitude, his very presence. 'Those stories of mine you took.'

Paul became serious. 'I'm sorry we didn't get a proper chance to discuss that,' he told me. 'The truth is, the money on offer was never what it said in the papers. There were some doubts about authenticity...'

He hesitated. I tried to keep a poker face. Did he know I'd forged them?

'The upshot is I haven't been paid yet. When I do, I'll send you half.'

'Half?' I stepped out of the boxroom and Paul followed me.

'Fifty-fifty's the usual deal on stuff like this.'

'Is that what you'll be charging Tony?' I asked, shutting the box room door.

'No. Tony's archive is fully documented and authenticated. That makes a great deal of difference in the rare manuscripts world. By the way, Mark...'

'Yes?'

'I presume your... friend doesn't know about the Paris manuscripts?'

'Not about my connection with them, no,' I replied, with

my back to him.

'I see.' He said nothing more, but followed me down the stairs. In the office, he greeted Tony ebulliently. 'I think we've got the makings of a great partnership. You know, you ought to have better security for your archives.'

'Mark's my watchdog,' Tony told Paul.

'How about I take you two for a meal? My treat?'

'Most kind.' Tony rarely turned down a free meal, but I hesitated. I had to set my discomfort against wanting to know how Paul would play Tony, what information he'd give to him. With Tony's weak bladder, there were bound to be further opportunities for me to press Paul about the Hemingway manuscripts. Also, I hadn't had a good meal in weeks.

'Are you coming, Mark?' Paul asked.

'If I'm welcome,' I said.

'Is there somewhere near you can suggest? Paul asked Tony.

'I'll give the French House a ring, see if they can fit us in.'

While Tony was on the phone, Paul looked at me appraisingly. His expression reminded me that we both knew something Tony didn't. It felt like a betrayal.

The small upstairs restaurant was crowded but Tony was a regular, so a table was soon found. Paul, at Tony's suggestion, ordered oysters and kidneys, a house speciality. I had oysters, too, since Paul was paying and I'd never had them before. I remember the slippery texture of the shellfish and the way it was spoilt for me by a smutty joke Paul made about the clitoris.

When Tony went downstairs to use the loo I challenged Paul about the manuscripts again.

'You had no right to sell those papers of mine.'

Paul was unflurried by my attack. 'I told you, Mark. They haven't been sold. That was publicity flim flam. You want them

149

back? I could get them. There'd be some explaining to do, which might be a little awkward for you, given your current position.'

'What do you mean?'

'You're responsible for an archive containing rare manuscripts by famous writers, a potential gold mine you don't want to compromise.'

'That's not why I'm...'

Paul laughed. 'Then why else are you here? Out of love?'

'Love? In a way.' Naively, I thought he meant love of literature, but I didn't get the chance to explain this.

'Let me ask you a question, Mark. How old are you?'

'I...'

'You see, I thought you were nearly the same age as Helen. That watch. Didn't we give it you for your twentieth birthday? But when Tony and I were talking before you arrived, your boss called you a very bright teenager. Is that part of your con, Mark? Getting Tony to think that you're younger than you are?'

'No.' This was such a minor fib that I decided to come clean. 'I lied about my age to Helen, so that she'd respect me more. I'm not twenty until March.'

'So what you and Tony are doing has to be kept hush hush.'

'I don't follow you.'

'Oh come on, Mark. It's obvious what you're up to. Tony can do you a lot of good. Get you published. Introduce you to the right people. Maybe he'll even put you in his will. Then there are all those rare papers. You should have seen the look on your face when you realised that I knew all about them.'

'You've got entirely the wrong end of the stick,' I said.

'Don't take me for a fool. Why else are you with Tony? It can't be for the sake of that crappy little room above the office. No doubt you spend most of your time at his flat.'

'I never...'

'Gay sex under the age of twenty-one is illegal in this country, isn't it?'

I began to stand. 'I don't. I'm not...'

Tony, returning from the toilet, saw that I was uncomfortable. 'Are you all right, old son?' he asked me.

'I don't think those oysters agreed with me.' Angry, I left the room. Tony had never made the slightest move on me. Paul, by contrast, was sick enough to seduce his own stepdaughter.

When I got back to the table, Paul was tucking into his kidneys. Between bites, he was telling Tony an anecdote about Roald Dahl and *Playboy* magazine. I realised that Tony must have mentioned *The Woman Who Married Herself.*

'*Playboy* published a lot of his stuff — cynical little things that appealed to jaded readers taking a break before they had the energy to jack off again. So Dahl publishes this story there — not long back, around eighty-seven or so: *The Bookseller*, I think it was called. It's a neat little idea. This bookseller goes through the obits, finding married men who've just died. And he sends the dead man a bill for magazines that are clearly hard core porn. The widow always pays up, to avoid any embarrassment. A neat scam. Only, one day, he tries to pull the trick on the widow of a blind man...'

Tony guffawed. I smirked. A typical Dahl plot, I thought, simple and satisfying. But then Paul added the second twist.

'So I read this story in *Playboy* and thought, hang on, I've seen this before. Sure enough, I track it down in some paperback anthology came out when I was a kid. *Clerical Error* was the original name. Only the author wasn't Dahl. He'd — what's the word you guys use? — nicked it. A whole bunch of people wrote to *Playboy* to point out where he'd stolen it from. The magazine protected him, didn't print any of the letters.'

I felt a surge of relief. Dahl, whom I had forged, was himself a plagiarist, though possibly an unconscious one. It made me feel better about what I'd done.

'What's this story of his you're using?' Paul asked.

'You tell it, Mark,' Tony said.

'I'd rather you did.'

So Tony told the story. He missed bits out, but got the essence of it. When he'd finished, Paul clapped his hands together.

'You don't recognise the story, I hope?' Tony asked, mildly teasing our American host.

'No, but I recognise a good property when I hear one. I'm surprised Dahl didn't dig that one out for *Playboy*. You know, it has serious movie potential. You're going to put it in your five hundredth issue?'

'Possibly.'

'I'll tell you what I'd do,' Paul said, and paused. Tony was carefully separating some sea bass from the bone, so he couldn't see the American's face. 'I'd take Dahl's name off that story,' Paul went on, 'put yours under it — or, even better...' Paul paused and winked at me. 'Use young Mark's name — and sell it to Hollywood. You'd cash in.'

'What an intriguing idea,' Tony said, as my blood froze. I understood the implications of that wink. My forgeries were no longer a secret.

Thirty-two

'What did you think of him?' Tony asked the next day. I had left the French House before they'd finished eating, claiming my stomach ache was worse.

'I didn't trust him,' I replied without hesitation. Tony smiled.

'Me neither, but he could be what we need. Why didn't you like him?'

'Too smooth, too well dressed.'

'I know what you mean. My father used to say you should be with someone at least a minute before you can tell that they're well dressed. Any sooner, and they're either a fop or a fraud. To be sure about Mercer, I made a couple of calls to friends in the States last night. They'd both heard of him. He married a stepdaughter half his age and there was a splash in the papers. Apart from that, the word is that Mercer knows his way about the literary manuscripts world. He's the man who found those Hemingway typescripts in Paris... do you remember my showing you the story in the *TLS*?'

I gave the smallest of nods and Tony continued.

'Mercer's handled some Joyce letters too. My friends reckon he has a good eye for authors who are likely to be collectable in the future. He wasn't over here to see me, you know. It was a flying visit to try and get VS Pritchett to flog him his first drafts. The old man told him to get stuffed so he popped in on us instead.'

Tony was impressed, I could see. How could Paul know so much about Literature, I wondered? He hadn't struck me as at all literary when we were in Paris. But then, he wasn't trying to impress me. One thing I was sure of: Paul was not a litterateur, he was a salesman, only in it for the money.

'He's made an offer for the entire archive. Seventy-five thousand pounds. That's pretty generous, wouldn't you say?'

I had no idea, and said so.

'According to him, there are three ways of going about it. I could put the lot up for auction, which might net me the most, but, if the right number of bidders didn't appear, might only raise ten or twenty thousand. I could sell the archive to a university using him as a middle man, for which he would expect fifteen or twenty per cent. But that would take several months. He reckoned that he could probably get a hundred thousand, more or less. Or I could sell the archive to him outright, for the seventy-five, and he would then sell it on when he thought the market was at its best. What do you think?'

I thought Paul was using the money he'd made from my Hemingway stories to buy up Tony's life's work, but I couldn't say this.

'If I were you,' I told him 'I'd get a second opinion.'

'That's in hand. A man from Christie's is coming tomorrow. But I'm inclined to sell the archive to Mercer outright. That way, I might lose a few thousand in the long run, but I'd get the final issue out more or less on time. The magazine's reputation wouldn't suffer.'

I noted that phrase 'final issue' and my heart sank.

'Is that it, then?' I asked Tony. 'Do you plan to close down?'

'I think so,' he said. 'We'll go out with a giant fuck you to the Arts Board: a staggering list of contents, top quality production and an introduction naming names, full of bile. What do you think?'

In a way it seemed appropriate that my forgeries should indirectly pay for the final issue of the *Little Review*, but I couldn't say this.

'I'd have thought you'd want to retire with something more dignified than a fart in the face of the Arts Board.'

154

'You're probably right,' Tony said, 'but allow me the luxury of imagining it for a while first.'

I didn't ask Tony the other question on my mind. What would happen to the office and my flat above? His lease ran until the end of 1994, which would have seen me comfortably to the end of my University career, if I made it that far. I supposed Tony would sell or sublet, but maybe I would be able to hang onto the flat. I was used to living in Soho, in the middle of things, even though my home was meagre and I couldn't afford to make much use of the West End's shops, theatres and restaurants. Now and then I got a cheap standby ticket for the theatre, or went along with Tony to a club or gallery. And I never bought books. Rather, I sold review copies for food and still had more than enough to read. All that would stop when the magazine closed down.

The other thing I'd miss was 'literary' London. I sometimes went to book launches and the like. Tony could no longer be bothered with them. The free food and drink were the main appeal, but they also gave me a glimpse of the world I aspired to join, one more glamorous and mysterious than the *Little Review*'s.

'When do you have to decide by?' I asked Tony.

'Mercer will be back in London in a week.'

'You mean he's already gone?'

'Back to New York on a morning flight, yes.'

My secret was safe for now.

'Going to the Richard Mayfield launch tonight, are you?' Tony asked, later, seeing the invitation I'd left on top of a pile of submissions. It was a book launch at the Groucho club. The club was only a stone's throw from our office, but I'd never been inside (you needed to be a member, or to be with one) and was interested in seeing it, especially as such invitations weren't likely to come my way for much longer.

'I think so.'

'I turned him down two or three times. Precocious brat. Talented, though. Be interested to see what you make of him.'

If Mayfield, with a novel published straight after he left university, was irritatingly precocious, what was I, who had been mistaken for Hemingway and Greene? When Tony left for home, I went upstairs, where I through the complicated business of having a thorough wash with only a small sink in which to do so. By the time I'd dried my hair and ironed my best clothes, the book launch would be under way.

Or so I thought. I showed up at the time advertised, presented my invitation at the door and was directed to a large room upstairs. I expected my customary clothing (black, black and black) to keep me anonymous. In London, outside the office, I always felt anonymous, more like a ghost than a participant. However, I was one of the first to arrive. As I reached for a glass, a sleek, skinny publicist pounced on me. She was also dressed entirely in black, though I knew the labels inside would shame my basement store bargains.

'Are you *The Face*?' she asked.

'No. I'm...'

'Dazed And Confused?'

'All the time,' I joked. No laugh. 'Is that a magazine?'

'Yes,' she said. This was already the longest conversation I'd sustained at a literary launch. I generally stood around, deliberately fading into the background, eating canapés, getting mildly drunk on free wine. But the woman didn't go away.

'I'm from the *LR*,' I said.

'London..?'

'Little Review.'

'Oh.' She glanced at the door with the classic look over the shoulder in search of someone more interesting, more useful.

This action was not considered rude, Tony told me once. Literature was, after all, a business, and we were the smallest fish in the sea. But hardly anybody had arrived yet, so she returned her attention to me.

'Would you like to meet the author?' she asked.

I wanted to say 'no', but could hardly say that I was only there for the free food.

'Which is he?' I asked.

She pointed towards a bloke in a velvet jacket who couldn't be much older than I was. Then she took my elbow and guided me towards him.

'Richard, I'd like you to meet Mark Trace, from the *Little Magazine.* He's a great admirer of your work.'

'She meant *Little Review,*' I corrected once the publicist had floated away.

'A *great admirer,* eh?' Richard Mayfield had long, curly hair and a frilly shirt beneath his scarlet smoking jacket. 'Such a great admirer that you bastards never published me.'

The intensity of the bitterness in his voice took me aback.

'I've only been working there for nine months,' I said. 'I don't recall any of your stuff coming through.'

'I stopped sending it out once I got a publishing contract,' Richard told me. Then he offered me his hand and I shook it. 'Sorry,' he said. 'These things make me edgy. I don't know what I'm doing here.'

He went silent and I realised that I had to make conversation. What to say? I hadn't read any of his books and certainly wasn't going to confront him with what Tony had said about him.

'Tony reckons that nobody serious writes anything interesting before they're thirty,' I said, and immediately worried that even this might sound insulting.

'So I have to wait another seven years before he'll publish

157

me?' Mayfield asked, his tone inquisitorial.

'I hope he's wrong,' I said. 'Otherwise I've got over a decade to go.'

'What do you do there?' the author asked.

'Editorial assistant. Archivist. Dogsbody. That kind of thing.'

'Published anything?'

'A couple of reviews.'

'And you're... what, twenty?'

'In a few weeks.'

'Come to many of these beanos?'

'Only for the free wine.'

The author smiled. 'A man after my own heart. Come on. Drain that and have another. I need to be pissed before I can read in front of people.'

As we refilled our drinks, the hordes arrived. We were quickly separated. Richard Mayfield gave a brief reading, which was well received, but impossible to concentrate on. The room was full of people who seemed to know each other. I recognised a few but not to talk to. After a few minutes, I realised that Richard was equally out of his depth. We gravitated towards each other. He asked how come I was working for the *LR* and I told him about being kicked out of university.

'Best thing that could happen to you,' he said. 'Doing a literature degree is stifling for a writer — all those influences to shake off, all that close analysis and academic bollocks. You'd never be able to write an unselfconscious word.'

This made sense to me. For the first time, I had doubts about returning to my course.

'What did you do at university?' I asked.

'Me? Oh, I read PPE.'

I somehow guessed that this meant he'd been to Oxford or Cambridge, which explained where he got the connections to be published at twenty-three. I had no idea what PPE stood for.

'What writers do you like?' I asked. The natural question.

He rattled off a few names, the great and trendy, and I nodded half heartedly. 'You know who I really rate?' he asked, 'the one I'd like to emulate, if I had half his ability?'

'No. Who?'

'James Sherwin.'

And from that point, of course, we were off, for he knew almost as much about James Sherwin as I did. Moreover, we both knew things the other didn't. I, for instance, was able to quote from a letter which Sherwin had written the month before. Richard knew a story about Sherwin's unfinished novel *A Commune* which might explain why it had never been finished.

'Story goes that there was a real commune on the island where Sherwin lived. That's where he got the idea. But while he was writing the book, somebody got murdered, or committed suicide, I don't know which. And Sherwin got spooked.'

'Where did you hear that?'

'I don't recall. I must have read it somewhere.'

We were still talking when the party emptied. Richard gathered up two opened but unfinished bottles of wine and we took them back to my room above the magazine.

'This is great!' he said, seeing my word processor propped on its rickety table by the bed. 'The ideal place for a writer. What are you working on?'

I hesitated. I couldn't tell him that I was writing my own version of the novel we had been discussing earlier.

'Nothing much,' I muttered. 'Exercise, scraps of autobiography, trying to find my voice, if you like.'

'That's creative writing class bullshit,' Mayfield told me,

swigging from one bottle and handing me the other, which was to obliterate my memory of the remainder of the evening. 'Nobody *finds their own voice*. They steal somebody else's and improve on it. Believe me.'

I did. The conversation continued at full pelt for a couple of hours, after which Richard staggered out for the last tube. I thought it was the beginning of a lasting friendship, one which would nurture me as a writer, but, as things turned out, I haven't spoken to him since.

Thirty-three

The following week, experts from auction houses looked over the material in the *LR*'s archive. Men in old fashioned suits gave cautious appraisals. To my surprise, it appeared that Paul Mercer's offer was on the generous side.

'This kind of thing is notoriously difficult to estimate,' said the literary manuscripts man from Sotheby's. 'You might be looking at fifty thousand.'

A draft agreement arrived from America. If Tony signed it, the archive and all new material received in the final months of the magazine would become Paul's property as soon as the last issue was published.

'I know you don't trust him,' Tony told me, 'but it's a very good offer.'

What was the catch? Paul either knew or strongly suspected that I'd forged the Dahl and Hemingway stories. He might even have guessed about Greene. Was he expecting me to do more forgeries to add to the value of his collection? If so, it wouldn't work. Now other people had seen the archive, I couldn't add fresh, valuable material, even if I were so inclined.

'About the flat,' Tony went on. 'I'll try to sublet the office without the flat above — I know you like living here. I can't promise, but whoever rents the office might want to keep you on because you're useful for security.'

'It doesn't matter,' I lied. 'I can always find somewhere.'

We went back to work on the final issue. I was writing a short history of the magazine that would appear in the review section, alongside an attempt to sell off as many back issues as possible. The issue was very nearly full. Most of the contents had been typeset. If James Sherwin himself had sent a new story we'd have been pushed to fit it in. The Dahl family hadn't responded to the set of proofs Tony had sent them. Doubtless it was too soon after the author's death for such considerations. According to Tony, this was fine.

'If they say nothing, we go ahead with the story. If they refuse to let us publish, we're screwed.'

Those nights, when Tony went home in the evening, I felt at sea. The little world I'd created for myself was coming to an end and I didn't know where I was going next. I wanted to throw myself into being a writer, but knew I wasn't ready. I didn't want to return to university, at least not to my old course. I was coming to the conclusion that studying literature only made me self conscious about my own writing. Literary history might be useful for my career as a forger but that, too, was over. I'd got away with it, I thought, by working instinctively and by being lucky. Luck such as I'd had couldn't last.

I was still writing my Sherwin story. I had to write. How else could I occupy the long evenings when I had no money, no real friends? Yet I had no faith in the story unfolding, no hope that it would lead anywhere but deeper into itself, into the nothingness that was pretending to write as another man.

Thirty-four

Spring arrived, but my attic room remained cold, requiring at least one bar of the electric fire to be on all the time. I was writing obsessively, venturing out little, not eating enough. Now and then, Tony would drag me out for a bite, but his lunches were mostly liquid. I was returning from a trip to the post office when I found a young woman in the office. Hearing me approach, she stood and gave me a confident, American smile. I saw an attractive, rich, married young woman with expensively layered hair. For a moment, she didn't recognise me, but I would never mistake her.

'Helen,' I said, keeping my cool. 'What brings you here?'

'Mark,' she said, kissing me on the cheek. 'You look older.'

I had grown my first beard, a fine fuzz of ginger hair to hide the adolescent acne that still plagued me. I was a week away from my twentieth birthday and gaunt from eating too little. I had, without yet realising it, started to become attractive to women my own age, as well as to Tony's licentious friends. I had developed a 'starving artist in his garret' look that appealed to a certain kind of romantic, though romantic was never a word I'd use to describe Helen Mercer.

'So do you,' I replied, then realised this wasn't always a compliment for a woman, so added 'better than ever', which was equally true. The sullenness and frustrated air she'd had about her in Paris were gone. I tried not to look at the expensive bands on the third finger of her left hand, supposing they were the key to her transformation.

'Thanks,' she said, then added, as if we were close friends. 'We've got a lot of catching up to do.'

'Where's Tony?'

'He and Paul have gone out to talk business. Tony was sure

you'd be back soon, so I said I'd wait for you.'

'But Tony doesn't know that I know you,' I pointed out.

'Nevertheless, he said you'd be happy to show me the sights. He thought we'd get on,' she told me with a full smile.

'How long are you here for?' I asked.

'A few days. Paul wants to tie up some deals. We might look at a property in Chelsea, if I decide I like London more than New York. Will you show me round?'

Despite having lived in London for a year and a half, I'd hardly been to any of the tourist attractions. It wasn't that they didn't interest me so much as I didn't want to admit to myself that they interested me. I lived here. I wasn't a tourist. And I couldn't afford to visit most of them. Accompanying Helen, however, would make me a guide, a host.

'I wanted to apologise about the way we left Paris,' she told me, as we set out into Soho. 'I tried to get in touch with you soon after, but you were gone.'

'I had to leave in a hurry myself,' I told her, giving a brief account of my expulsion. Helen grimaced as she laughed.

'And I tried to persuade you to seduce her. I feel to blame. You must forgive me for that, too.'

I forgave her. Who would not forgive a beautiful woman when she was slipping her arm through his?

'Paul's nearly wrapped up the Hemingway deal,' she told me. 'He asked me to give you this, an advance of a thousand pounds.'

She handed me a handsome, pigskin wallet, stuffed with more twenty pound notes than I'd ever seen before.

'I chose the wallet,' Helen said. 'It's a gift. Do you like it?'

'It's... wonderful.' I kissed her on the cheek, as she had kissed me earlier.

'It's so good to see you again. You wouldn't believe how few people I know who are my own age.'

'Me too,' I said. Had Paul told her that I'd lied about my age, that I was three years younger than she was, rather than one? Probably. It didn't matter. We were much closer in age than Helen and her husband. We were in London on a beautiful spring day and I had a thousand pounds in my wallet.

Over the next few days, we went to galleries, parks and shops. Helen tried on endless tops, dresses and shoes. She insisted on buying a jacket and shirt for me: a reward for my escort duties. I bought myself a new pair of shoes with my 'advance'.

During these days, I didn't see Paul at all. I saw little of Tony, either, though I gathered that the archive deal was going ahead. Ridiculous though I knew it was, I found myself falling for Helen all over again. She was the first woman I'd ever really wanted. Her marriage only made me want her more. For what did Paul have that I didn't? Money. And he owed me a lot of that. He was fat and old, while I was young and good looking. Talented, too, I told myself. I would win out.

If I had been in love with London before, it was with a cramped, historic, archaic, literary London, a city I created more from my imagination than from what I saw around me. Now, on warm days at the beginning of spring, before the worst of the tourist rush began, with Helen gushing about how there was no place in the world like this and she ought to know, she'd been everywhere, I fell for the whole, unwieldy city in a big way.

I'd never talked to any friend as much as I talked to Helen that week. I told her my whole life story, bar the forgeries. After I'd told her about my mother, she told me about hers. It was a sad story and I got it in snatches while we were walking through town or sitting in restaurants, pubs and parks. Helen kept closing up, but I would ask another question and another until, slowly, it all came out.

Helen's mother had her when she was very young. Helen's father was a journalist who used to work with Paul Mercer on a New York listings magazine. The marriage lasted two years and Helen couldn't remember a thing about him.

'I haven't seen my dad since the day he walked out on Mom. Paul picked up the pieces. Paul was the only dad I ever got along with, but I hardly remember those days either. I was five when Mom left him. She moved in with this artist who was hot at the time. I don't even remember his second name. He means nothing now. My mother moved from man to man, always thinking the next one would give her what she wanted. The third one she married was a banker called Sam. He sent me away to school. I was brought up by nuns, can you believe that? Mom and Sam had an open marriage, so it lasted a little longer. But they fought because Sam wanted kids and Mom had had enough of that with me.

'Mom decided that all she wanted was to travel. She started getting into all sorts of spiritual shit. One time she came over to my school and tried to persuade me to drop out, go and live with her in an ashram. But I wanted education. I knew I needed something for myself because I couldn't rely on anyone else. Then, when I was fourteen, Mom went away and didn't come back. Sam supported me until I was eighteen, even though he didn't have to. He'd divorced Mom when I was sixteen. She'd abandoned both of us.

'After that, I was on my own. I moved to New York and was doing university courses, waiting tables, living in a hovel, when I bumped into Paul. Paul was separated, coming out of his fourth marriage. He was in rough shape, but he wanted to help. He offered me a home. He certainly didn't set out to seduce me. Still, one day it happened. We got together. His wife found out and set the police on us. So we decided to leave the country until Paul's divorce was final and I turned twenty-one. We'd been on the run six months when we met you.'

'I still find it hard to think of you as a couple,' I told her, cautiously. 'I mean, you were introduced to me as Paul's daughter.'

'We had no choice but to lie. Paul had to stump up for two bedroom suites wherever we stayed in case his wife's private detectives tracked us down. As far as the law was concerned, Paul was still my foster father, because Sam never adopted me. It was a vindictive divorce. His ex wanted to really rub his face in the dirt, create a scandal.'

It was a scandal, I thought, but I restricted myself to a question.

'Can you really be happy, married to a man twice your age?'

Helen gave me a smile that was almost patronising. 'In Paris, I told you about some of the guys I'd been out with. They were scum bags, users. Yes, there are nice things about younger guys, but there are nice things about older guys, too. Not least that they have more money, more experience. And Paul's a modern man. If I want to have a fling, I'm free to. We agreed that from the start.'

'And what if the guy you're with wants more than a fling?' I asked.

Helen didn't answer this, so I put my life into her hands. I kissed her.

She let my lips touch hers, but she didn't kiss back and, after a moment, I pulled away.

'Mark,' she said, 'you're my only real friend. Don't let's spoil that for...'

She didn't need to fill in the rest of the sentence. I wasn't after a fling. I wanted to go to bed with her more than I

167

wanted almost anything else, but I wanted much more than that. All I said was 'I care about you.'

'I care about you, too,' she said, and kissed me on the lips. It was more than a peck, but no more of a kiss than I'd allowed myself. She was making us even.

'Can you show me the British Library now?' she asked.

Thirty-five

As the week came to an end I saw less of Helen. She and Paul went to look at houses, though Helen said all they needed was an apartment.

'Paul's got this idea about us having children soon,' she told me, casually. 'I could imagine what that would be like — he'd still be going round the world all the time, doing deals, while I'd be at home looking after our brats in some dump where I don't know anybody. No thanks.'

There was work to be done on the magazine, too: checking proofs, chasing ads. Several of our regulars were putting in 'so long, it's been nice to know you' notices. It remained to be seen how many of these ads would be paid for. Tony was well aware that once the magazine was declared dead, he would have great difficulty getting his invoices paid. I had to take corrected copy to the printers, where I collected a new set of rejection slips. Most 'writers' who submitted work to magazines didn't buy the journals they wanted to be in. If they did, good magazines would turn a handsome profit, rather than requiring Arts Board grants. Submissions would continue to arrive for years after the *LR* closed. Those that enclosed a stamped, self addressed envelopes would receive the following:

> The Little Review *ceased publication with its five hundredth issue in April, 1991. Thank you for your interest and support over the years. The Editor wishes you well with your future writing. Back issues are still available. See the enclosed list.*

The deal with Paul Mercer was more or less complete and a for rent sign had appeared outside the office window. The owner of the porn shop downstairs had already been for a good look around, though he kept his intentions hazy.

'I don't know how I feel about this place becoming a peep show or a knocking shop,' Tony said. 'It would certainly ruin my chances of their mounting a blue plaque outside after I kick the bucket.'

We had a double blow. Both letters arrived in the same post. Roald Dahl's agent absolutely refused to allow his story to be published until he had had time to examine the manuscript and Dahl's records.

'Hardly surprising,' Tony said, after showing me the letter. 'If they're willing for it to be published, they might as well sell it somewhere that pays real money. Shame.'

But the next letter was completely unexpected. It was postmarked Greece.

'Sherwin?' I asked, as I handed Tony the letter, but he shook his head.

'Not his handwriting.'

It was from James Sherwin's wife, Sonia.

Dear Mr Bracken,

I write with sad news. James had a heart attack and died five days ago. We buried him yesterday in the small olive grove above our home. I know that you were old friends and he would have wanted you to be the first to know.

In sorting through my husband's recent correspondence, I see that you wrote asking for a piece for your five hundredth issue. Did he send you something? I can find no copy of his reply to you and James was always very secretive about his writing. If he did, I would be grateful to receive a copy. I am his literary executor.

May I ask you one final favour? Could you inform the media of James' death? I will write to his publishers. I expect that I will have to visit London soon and there ought to be some kind of memorial service. For the moment, however, I can't face these things.

Yours sincerely,
Sonia Sherwin

170

As I watched Tony mourn his old friend, my mind began to race. The thoughts I had did me no credit at all.

'Are you going to call the papers?' I asked, when he lifted his head.

'Tomorrow will do,' Tony said. 'A day will give me time to work on an obituary.'

Tony was often asked to write prepared obituaries, but he was superstitious, and would only write about people after they had died.

'I'm going to the Colony to get pissed,' he told me. 'We'll hold the space left by Dahl for a tribute to James. It won't sell as well, but he deserves it. Shut the office if you want. There's bugger all to do here now anyway.'

With that, he left, and I locked up, returning to my upstairs room to examine the story I'd been writing for months.

There were fifteen thousand words: three times the length of the average *LR* short story. Maybe I could fillet something decent out of them. I knew how much space there was and I knew which were the best pages of what I'd written. If I compressed those, I could make a reasonable stab at Sherwin. And I had a huge advantage. Sherwin used the same cheap word processor and printer that I did. Once I printed my work off, there was no way that the world's greatest forgery expert could tell the difference between my pages and ones printed in Greece. I was meant to do this.

Tony knew that Sherwin had sent no story. There was no way I could 'discover' one in the archives. I would have to tell Tony about my forgeries, which would mean coming clean about Dahl, and Greene, and possibly Hemingway, too. I wrote and rewrote the Sherwin passage, trying to ignore my dilemma. Once I did think about it, however, I realised something: I needed to tell Tony. I had to tell someone and I wanted to get the whole thing off my chest before he finalised the deal with Paul Mercer. Moreover, I wanted Tony to approve what I'd done.

Thirty-six

For nearly twenty years, James Sherwin has been one of the missing men of English Literature. Now he is lost forever. I vividly recall reading what was to be his first published short story, 'Silent Gunner'. It arrived on my desk in 1964, part of the ever growing post-bag of the small magazine I edited. Finding a talented author you'd never heard of was then — still is — a delightful surprise. I invited Jim to lunch, expecting someone my own age, finding instead a freckle-faced twenty-three year old who took his writing as seriously as only a very young man can.

He was an orphan, his parents having died in the war (father in Egypt, mother in a London air raid). For the next ten years, Jim was passed around between relatives. He was also an autodidact who left school at fifteen and worked menial jobs (park keeper, street-sweeper, bricklayer) that allowed him time to think and write.

Jim wrote in no recognisable tradition. He used to talk about Hemingway and Borges, but his favourite books were Bleak House *and* Vanity Fair. *For all the mysterious edginess of his prose, he was a storyteller at heart, and success came quickly. His work in magazines was noticed and written about even before his first novel, the semi-autobiographical* I, Singer *was published in '67. Then, at 26, he became — albeit briefly — a celebrity, feted by John Lennon and Mick Jagger, dating models and movie stars, gushingly reviewed wherever he was published. It was enough to turn anybody's head. James ceased being Jim, turning himself into a legend. James immersed himself in the subculture of sex, drugs and rock and roll. Now and then he would clear his head with trips to a remote Greek island, where he could be anonymous, recover and write.*

Fame did his writing no favours. All but one of the nine stories featured in his second book, User, *were written before this great success. It didn't matter. The book's publication both confirmed his reputation and raised expectations.*

However, James, always a slow writer, was drying up. His third and final book, Stargazer *was a novella of fewer than thirty thousand words. Like* I, Singer, *it told of a young man's disenchantment* with the material world. Where the singer sought refuge in surrealism, sex and wild antics, the star gazer opted for mysticism, an ascetic life, becoming first a drop out, then a recluse. This was 1970. Sales and reviews were less good than for I, Singer, but still healthy. James embarked on a reading tour of universities — first in Britain, then in the USA, where he befriended writers such as Donald Barthelme and Richard Brautigan. Rather than read from his earlier books, Sherwin would perform passages from a work in progress, A Commune.

The rest was silence. Sherwin retreated to the island of Karenos, where acolytes would try to track him down, usually failing. He wrote, farmed a little and meditated. A letter would come every few months. In the early ones, he talked about writing, but that soon stopped. Eventually, the letters slowed down to a trickle. Six years ago, he mentioned that he had married: 'a sweet American girl who wants to get me writing again'. But despite Sonia's encouragement, A Commune never appeared. When I wrote to him recently, asking for a piece for the Little Review's final issue, James wrote back 'Sonia bought me this computer in the hope that it would get me writing again, but all I seem to write on it are replies to prissy American doctoral students telling them to fuck off. Most days though, I sit down at the damned machine, try.'

James's death, of a heart attack, a few weeks after his fifty-third birthday, is a great loss. He was young still and might yet have finished the masterpiece many expected of him. Even so, he gave us two novels and ten enigmatic, exciting stories as good as anything written since the war. He is survived by his wife Sonia. They had no children.

'What do you think?' Tony asked me, after I'd read the obituary.

'It reads well,' I said, thinking. 'Shouldn't it have a bit more on his parents, background, that sort of thing?'

'I suppose so,' Tony told me. 'I could look all that stuff up.'

'No need,' I said. 'I've been researching Sherwin.'

I told Tony everything he needed, and more. He made

notes, then typed the changes into the computer.

'I didn't know you'd become such an expert,' he said. 'I'll print this off and fax it to *The Guardian*,' he said.

'Wait,' I told him. 'There's something you need to see first.'

I handed him the story I'd been working on.

'What is it?' Tony asked, glancing at the Ms. 'Trying to get another of your friend's stories in the magazine?'

Half the stuff we got from new writers — including Tim — was done on one of these Amstrads, with their slightly blurred dot matrix printouts.

'It's the same printer as James Sherwin used,' I said.

'I remember,' Tony told me, taking the manuscript from me, reading the title. *A Commune: extract from a work in progress*. His eyes widened. 'When did this arrive?'

I considered lying. I could say that it had come in the post with one of those envelope destroyed labels and no accompanying note, that I'd only just worked out what it was. But I'd lied too much already.

'It didn't,' I said.

'Maybe you found it in the archive,' Tony suggested, his voice unusually quiet. 'Something you missed earlier.'

'No,' I told him. 'I wrote it myself.'

'Ah.' Tony sat back, put his feet up on the desk and, ignoring me, began to read. I couldn't watch him, so I stared out of the window. The weather was warming up. Men were wearing jackets instead of coats. The girl from the CD shop down the road, whom I sometimes fantasised about, had on a short sleeved T-shirt. I watched her rearranging the two for ten pounds boxes on the stall outside the shop and remembered what my mother told me about *A Commune*, how it was meant to be the definitive account of how the sixties' dream went sour. How could I write about the sixties? I wasn't born until 1971.

Forty minutes later, Tony finished.

'How long did this take you?'

'A long time.'

'Longer than the others?' he asked, bluntly.

'Yes.'

Had he known before, or did he work it out while reading? I'd expected a big scene, but Tony was subdued. I couldn't tell if he was disappointed in me.

'Where did you learn to do this?' he asked.

'It's a long story.'

'I don't have anywhere I have to be.'

I told him — hesitantly at first, starting with Dickens in school, finishing with breaking into Dahl's writing hut. As I recounted this last story, Tony burst into laughter and I knew that, however wrong I might have been, I was forgiven.

'The irony is,' he said when he'd recovered, 'that's the best one. Oh dear...'

His eyes had watered. He wiped them, then said, 'what am I going to tell Graham?'

'I don't know.'

'He suspected, you know. That was what first made me suspicious. I didn't read out all of his letter to you. Let me find it.'

He unlocked the top drawer of his desk, found the Greene letter and handed it to me. I read the familiar words, then got to the paragraph that Tony hadn't included when he read it aloud.

From the photocopy, this looks right, but I have no recollection whatsoever of writing it. Was I overdoing the benzedrine at the time? The style's rather ragged, and that might explain it. Or is it possible somebody's pulling a fast one on you? If I remember correctly, St. Pancras was railway offices at the time, not closed down, which seems an odd mistake for me to make. Publish by all means, if you think it's good enough. I'm afraid I'm not up to doing a rewrite at the moment.

I handed the letter back.

'I wasn't a hundred percent sure,' Tony told me. 'It seemed far too good for a nineteen year old, and the story was a god-send, so I wasn't inclined to challenge it. Then Roald Dahl died and I decided to set you a test.'

'You knew I'd faked the Dahl story?'

Tony gave me one of his supercilious looks. 'You didn't know Dahl. He wouldn't have left even a bad story lying around for forty years. He'd have recycled it. That's what writers do.'

'There's somebody you haven't mentioned,' I said, meaning Sherwin, but Tony started talking about Paul Mercer instead.

'I couldn't understand why he'd alighted on me and was overpaying for the archives. Then I discovered that he was the man who'd sold those Hemingway papers. And I put two and two together. You were in Paris when those stories were discovered. Ergo, Mercer got them from you. Mercer found me thanks to you.'

'I wrote to him,' I explained. 'I wanted to know what had happened to the money from the stories. Last week he told me that they still weren't sold.'

'Bollocks,' Tony told me. 'The man's a con artist. I don't know what his game is and I doubt that I'll see the seventy-five thousand he's promised me. I'm interested to find out, that's all. Have you slept with his wife yet?'

'No!'

'Why not? Don't tell me she's faithful to him.'

'No. I mean, she doesn't have to be. It's just...'

'You've got her to yourself most days. What are you waiting for? You should take every opportunity that presents itself, otherwise you'll end up with nothing but regrets.'

It was hard to explain that Helen preferred me as a friend. Tony couldn't understand how any man could fail to be completely controlled by his cock. I mumbled something then said what was really on my mind.

'What did you think of the Sherwin story?'

'Not bad,' Tony told me. 'Needs work. You know, I heard Jim reading some of *A Commune* in 1970. If I looked in my diary, I might have some notes on what it was about.'

'Do you really want me to do some work on the story?' I asked, still unsure what Tony was thinking.

'Why not?' Tony asked again. 'Jim's dead. It won't hurt him where he is. The wife's probably short of money. It'll give her something to show publishers, and we'll sell more copies of the magazine, too. But we have to make sure it's good enough. How fast can you write?'

'Pretty fast,' I replied.

'Good. Because it's imperative that the issue goes to press by the end of the week. Now, how shall I rewrite the penultimate paragraph for *The Guardian*? Let's see. *When I wrote to him recently, asking for a piece for the* Little Review's *final issue, James wrote back 'Sonia bought me this computer in the hope that it would get me writing again, but all I seem to write on it are replies to prissy American doctoral students telling them to fuck off. Most days though, I sit down at the damned machine, try. See what you think of this.* Does that sound convincing?'

'Sure,' I said. 'But you'll have to explain what "this" is.'

Tony began to type. *'This' was an extract from* A Commune, *showing that he was still working on the book, twenty years on. The material he sent will appear in the final issue of the* Little Review, *to be published next month.*

'And then as before. What do you think?'

'Great,' I said. 'Let's do it.'

Only when he'd sent it off did I think of a complication. 'If you're selling the archive, then Paul will get the Sherwin letter and the manuscript.'

'He can have them. We'll print off a second copy of the story for the wife,' Tony told me. 'As for the letter...'

He found Sherwin's original letter in the drawer and looked at the signature, then at the writing on the envelope.

'Two choices. Either I hand write the extra words in blue-black ink. Or you retype the whole letter on your computer, print it off, and I forge the signature. What do you think?'

I thought about it. 'It's possible the wife will find the original letter on his computer and discover it was changed. Better to hand write the extra note, if you can do it convincingly.'

'I'll practise,' Tony told me, with a mischievous grin. He was getting into the game. 'Go to Ryman's. Buy me as many different kinds of blue-black ink as they sell.'

When I returned, Tony showed me his imitation of Sherwin's writing. He played about with ink until he'd got the right shade. Then, taking a deep breath, he wrote the note onto Sherwin's original letter. His hand jerked at one moment and I thought that he was going to lose it. But the words, as they appeared, looked convincing. *See what you think of this.* We watched the ink dry then compared the colour with that of the signature.

'It looks right,' I told Tony.

'Let's hope so. Now, we have to get on with your story.'

'I could bring the word processor down and we could work in here.'

'No,' Tony told me. 'Mercer may show up any time. The deal's meant to be signed tomorrow. I don't want him to see anything suspicious. Let's move your computer to my flat. We can work on it there.'

'I'll book a taxi to take it. I've got to meet Helen in a few minutes, but I'll join you there.'

'Bring a change of clothes. You might need to work all night.'

178

Thirty-seven

'I thought you'd stood me up,' Helen said, outside Buckingham Palace, where she'd been watching the Changing of the Guard.

'Sorry,' I told her. 'A writer's died. We need to remake the final issue. What was it like?'

'OK,' Helen said. 'What writer? Anyone I'd have heard of?'

'I doubt it,' I said, hooking my arm through hers. 'A guy from the sixties, James Sherwin.'

Helen blinked. We began to walk. 'He wrote *Stargazer*, yeah?'

'Yeah.'

'My mum was keen on that book.'

'Mine too.'

'Where are we going?' Helen asked.

'I don't know. Just walking, I guess. What do you want to do?'

'Nothing special,' Helen said. 'I like just walking with you.'

'Fine. We'll stop when we see somewhere we want to go into. What did you do last night?'

'Paul took me to Simpsons-on-the-Strand. I was the youngest person there by years. Come to think of it, Paul was the second youngest person there.'

We laughed.

'You have to work tonight?' she asked.

'I'm afraid so. The last issue has to be ready to print by next week.'

'Tomorrow's my last night before we go back to New York.'

'What are you doing?'

'Nothing,' Helen told me. 'Paul's got to go to Scotland. He's negotiating to buy some Robert Louis Stevenson papers. He tried to persuade me to go with him but it's cold up there. I'd prefer to be here, with you. Let me buy you dinner tomorrow night to thank you for showing me round these last few days.'

'I'd love that,' I said.

We discussed where to eat and arranged to meet at her hotel. Our wandering had somehow brought us back to Soho.

'You're so lucky,' Helen said, 'living in the heart of things.'

'It's not as romantic as it seems,' I told her. 'A bit of a hovel, really.'

'I've never seen your room,' Helen said, leaning into me as she spoke. 'Will you show me?'

'If you like,' I said, trying to remember what kind of state I'd left it in.

'Will Tony be there?'

'No. He's gone home for the day.' And I was meant to be with him soon, but I didn't tell Helen this. She followed me up to the office, then held onto my arm as we climbed the rickety stairs to my tiny flat.

'It's so small!' she said. 'Is this where you do your writing?'

'Mostly. I sometimes use the office, but, at night, when the heat's off, it's easier to get this room warm.'

'What do you use? A typewriter?'

'Pen and ink,' I lied, not wanting to explain where my computer had gone. But Helen had moved on to something else. She bounced on my three-quarter sized bed.

'A big bed for such a small room.'

'Tony used to use it for his assignations.'

'Tony, but not you?'

Scarcely knowing how to reply, I stood at the window. I pointed to a building two doors down.

'Graham Greene used to meet a prostitute called Pepe in that room. There's a story about it in the last issue but one.'

'And you?' Helen asked again. Her hand stroked my back. 'Do you ever..?'

I put my arm around her shoulders and she didn't flinch from my touch.

'I know some of the working girls. They say hello, but that's all. I've been waiting...'

'I know you have,' Helen said, and her touch changed. Her hand started to slide into the back of my jeans. Gently, I turned her towards me. We kissed.

It wasn't like the enthusiastic but inexperienced kisses I'd shared with Francine. It was a carnal kiss. Our bodies rubbed against each other so hungrily, I thought we might make love then and there. But we didn't.

'I've got to go,' Helen told me, breathlessly. 'Paul's expecting me. I'll see you tomorrow.'

With that, she hurried out, not even giving me time to say goodbye. It seemed that Tony, this morning, had been right about Helen, as about so many other things. She was mine for the taking.

When I got to Highgate I found that Tony had set up my computer in the living room. He had a pot of coffee on the go.

'By the time the obituaries appear in the morning, we've got to have a convincing Sherwin story ready,' he told me.

The news of Sherwin's death had only just broken in the media. The BBC's Ceefax service had two sentences saying that Greek authorities had confirmed the death of British born author James Sherwin, at the age of fifty-three. As we worked into the evening, Tony put on the Radio Four programme *Kaleidoscope*, which ran a brief item about Sherwin's death.

'It's almost twenty years since he disappeared from the literary scene, but author James Sherwin, whose death was announced today, casts a long shadow. Twenty-four years since his only full length novel *I, Singer*, Sherwin's many fans are still awaiting a successor. Now that he's dead, the question is: will his readers have to wait forever?'

Two Sherwin 'scholars' debated this issue (they had no idea) then moved on to place James Sherwin's place in history. The first said that he deserved to be talked about in the same breath as Borges or Kafka. The other thought he'd been overrated, perhaps because he published so little, when he was so young.

'There's bound to be a flood of posthumous publications, and then we'll see. My guess is that the Sherwin bubble will burst and he'll soon be little more than a sixties footnote...'

'Should we be doing this?' I asked Tony, as the item ended.

'How do you mean?'

'Whatever I do, however good it is, we'll be messing with his reputation.'

'James didn't give a fig what happened after he was dead,' Tony assured me. 'He didn't believe in a personal afterlife and a literary afterlife wouldn't have interested him either. He'd have enjoyed the joke.'

Tony showed me some notes he'd made at the last reading he saw Sherwin give. The details were scant. *James read a passage about hippies living in caves on an island. Broad comedy at first, unusual for him. Hints of more characteristic darkness towards the end.*

'It's too dangerous,' I told Tony. 'The stuff I've already written is based on so little information. Somebody might have taped his readings. In America, they almost certainly did. We'll be caught out.'

'Yet you tell me you've been trying to write the book he wrote.'

'Or would have written,' I explained to Tony. 'I thought he'd given up writing altogether. But what I wrote was an exercise, for myself, not for publication. The part I showed you is the best bit.'

We agreed to look at my piece together, seeing what worked and what didn't. It was an absorbing process. We examined each paragraph in detail, line by line, word by word. The only thing Tony left alone was the punctuation. I found it easy to imitate any writer's punctuation habits. I knew all about Sherwin's over-use of colons, his misuse of commas, his chaotic way with italics, his preference for the dash over parentheses.

Examining my story with Tony, I felt like I was learning more than ever before. His questions were very simple. 'Why would he use that word? What's he trying to say here?' We examined the story as though it were by Sherwin himself and we, his editors, were trying to decipher his wishes.

'Have you done this before?' I asked Tony at one point. 'Did you go over the two stories of Sherwin's that you published with him?'

'Not as closely as this,' Tony said. 'But, yes. I asked some questions. Jim made a few minor changes as a result. Great writers rarely mind being edited. All they want is for their work to be as good as possible.'

We worked for hours, losing track of time. Now and then I had a breakthrough. A sentence or two disappeared. A paragraph was moved to a different place. A new line of dialogue lifted the story, giving hints of a meaning that shifted the ground in a typically elliptical way. I worked in a reference to living in caves, which anyone who remembered Sherwin's readings of nineteen years before might notice and say — *ah, yes, it comes back to me now.* By the early hours of the morning, we were as near as we were going to get.

'I suggest we sleep on it,' Tony said, pouring us both a large scotch. 'See how it looks in the morning.'

He made me up a bed on the sofa, then retired. It took me a while to get off. I was exhilarated by the work I'd done. It was the most demanding forgery I'd done, written in the full knowledge that what I wrote would be subjected to endless scrutiny. Yet, thanks to Tony's help, I felt confident.

'It's a funny thing,' Tony said to me at midday, when I was halfway through my second mug of tea. 'You hear of paintings being forged all the time, but never literature. Why? I've been wondering. Because there's so little demand? Hardly. Because it's hard to do convincingly? Surely not. Experts are easy to fool. Think of the Hitler diaries and the nobs who were taken in by them. I think it's because writing great literature requires both enormous skill and immense talent. Painting skills are easily picked up. You can get by on a little talent and a lot of application. The painter is valued for originality, for innovation. Copying somebody else's innovations is relatively easy. But literature has to remake itself all the time. The writer himself often falls short of the mark. Every now and then an obscure academic tries to make a name for himself by attributing some long lost poem or play to Shakespeare. He may be right. We'll never know. But people don't want to believe the attribution because the piece simply isn't good enough.'

'What are you getting at?' I asked. 'You want me to forge Shakespeare?'

'No. You've been careful to do twentieth century writers, forging in an area where it's still possible to create a patina of reality in the manuscripts. You're able to mimic the minds of men who are nearly your contemporaries. That's the clever thing. I don't understand how you do it. Talent, sure, but it's a special skill, too. Lots of writers copy others. But you become them. It's a kind of genius. I wonder how long you'll be able to do it.'

This was a question I often asked myself. In a way, I didn't want my facility for forgery to last. I wanted my writing to become itself, not a copy.

'Perhaps it's like having a photographic memory,' Tony went on, 'something a few people have when they're young, but which quickly fades in adulthood. You never know. Could be it's a skill you'll always possess. The only way to find out would be to locate other people who've shared the same skill. But if others existed, then, by the very nature of the thing, we wouldn't know who they were.'

The phone rang, interrupting our conversation. Tony answered.

'Paul, how are you? Yes, tomorrow is fine. I'll sign the papers today, so that we can meet at your solicitors when you return. Have a good trip.'

He put the phone down, then told me, with a sly smile, 'According to Paul Mercer, I should get my seventy-five thousand tomorrow.'

We went over the Sherwin story one more time, then Tony printed off two copies: one for the typesetters, one for Sonia Sherwin. Before leaving, I went and bought the day's broadsheets. We wanted to read the Sherwin obituaries. Tony's was the best informed. The paper had added tributes from JG Ballard and Michael Moorcock. Elsewhere, *The Independent* wrote that Sherwin was one of the most original British novelists to emerge since the war. *The Times* was more niggardly, describing Sherwin as a sixties casualty who 'had the good grace to disappear, rather than continue trading on his inflated reputation. He will be remembered, if at all, for the minor curiosity that is *I, Singer*, a book often begun but seldom finished by a generation of aspirant dropouts.' *The Daily Telegraph* didn't cover Sherwin's death at all, giving all their space to two ex-army men and a senior figure from the British Medical Council.

Reading these obituaries, I worried again about how my story would affect posterity's view of Sherwin. But Tony told me I was wrong.

'Interest in writers tends to wane when they die. Their books turn up cheap in the secondhand shops. Nobody wants to write about them. Most sink back into the obscurity they came from. Few rise again. We're helping to keep Jim in the public eye. Don't feel guilty about it.'

I noticed that Sherwin had become 'Jim' again. In death, Tony was able to reclaim the old friend whose work he'd discovered. Tony called a taxi. We loaded the computer, then rode to Soho, dropping the story off to be typeset on the way. The final issue was ready to go to press.

'Paul's spending the night in Scotland,' Tony told me, as I struggled upstairs with my trusty Amstrad. 'His young wife will be all alone. Just in case you wanted to know.'

Thirty-eight

I was in a chipper mood when I collected Helen, wearing the clothes she'd helped me choose (and mostly paid for). My beard was trimmed, my hair washed. I was anxious to keep Helen to her half promise of the afternoon before. But Helen, while affectionate, seemed ill at ease. She was dressed young, in jeans, trainers, and a sliver of a silk top concealed beneath the khaki combat jacket that half the young women in London seemed to wear that year. Yet her face was lined with concerns she didn't share with me. Our conversation was aimless, arbitrary, as though we were both putting off the real point of our evening.

After the meal we walked, arms tentatively linked, along the Charing Cross Road. Some of its secondhand bookshops were still open, even though it was after ten. Helen insisted on going in to Any Amount of Books, where she asked for a copy of *User*, Sherwin's book of short stories.

'Sorry. We had one, but it went earlier today. The book's still in paperback, I think.'

It was, and I had my mother's copy back at the office, but I didn't mention this to Helen, any more than I mentioned the Sherwin story about to appear in our final issue. I was beginning to doubt what had grown between us that week, to see how little, really, we had in common. Helen was a married woman from another country. I was a callow youth, inexperienced, a virgin. What happened later was bound to disappoint her and might humiliate me. My half plan, to ask her to leave Paul, to stay here with me, seemed ridiculous. What would Helen want with a penniless nineteen year old who had no proper home or job?

We were near the office. I would be more at ease there than

in a hotel room paid for by Paul. Also, If Helen refused to come up, I would know there was no chance. I would see her to the door of her hotel then walk back.

'We're right by my flat,' I said. 'Let's go there.'

Helen didn't look at me. 'It's not much further to the hotel,' she said.

'You spend most of your life in hotels,' I told her. 'Come to the flat. There's a bottle of whisky in the office.'

'There's a mini-bar in the room,' Helen told me. 'I'd feel more comfortable there, Mark. Please.'

That *please* did it. In silence, we walked along the Strand. When we got to the hotel, the doormen in their top hats and Victorian coats were enough to intimidate me.

'I don't belong in there,' I told Helen.

'You must come in,' she said, insistently.

'No. Let's say goodbye here,' I told her.

'I don't want to say goodbye,' she said, then kissed me fully on the mouth.

I wavered and she took my hand, guiding me towards the glass door that glided open for us. We crossed the lobby and were in the lift, alone, kissing again. Helen's hands were all over me. Too eager. She had become the awkward one.

How many times since have I replayed in my head what happened next? The room is huge, with two beds, which is a relief because it allows me to think that Helen and Paul don't sleep in the same bed, that they haven't had sex in either one. Helen gets a bottle of champagne from the mini-bar and I'm all for opening it right away but Helen tells me to wait. So we kiss and caress and completely undress. Horniness makes me commandeering or maybe it's that Helen is so submissive I feel able to thrust myself on her but she's experienced and knows how to stop me from entering her and it's just starting to occur to me that maybe this is some enormous set up and

Paul is going to walk in at any moment freshly arrived from Scotland and shoot me or something like that when I hear Big Ben in the distance, chiming midnight and Helen is out from under me, removing the champagne from the fridge. As the last chime sounds, the glasses are full and, resplendently naked, she holds one out to me and says 'Happy Birthday'.

I am twenty years old. My birthday is something I've avoided thinking about since Helen told me she'd be gone by today and she will be gone but right now she's here, giving me champagne kisses, telling me it's time for my present, and I'm amazed that she's remembered, after all it's been nearly two years and I ask her what my present is, although I already know.

Afterwards, Helen pours the last of the chilled champagne, tells me I must take a bath with her. We get into the large, freestanding bath, filled with bubbles that begin to overflow onto the tiles below, and we sip champagne while washing each other. Now that I'm sated with sex, brilliant sex, Helen no longer seems older than me. She is only very beautiful, and vulnerable. And later, when we are holding each other in bed, I try to talk to Helen about the future, and leaving her husband. But she puts her finger to my lips and we begin to make love for a second time that threatens to last forever, yet doesn't.

Then Helen is sleeping, but I'm not. I'm wide awake. I want to shout, and sing, and I pull out my notebook and fill it with nonsense, all about Helen. Then I try to sleep, but can't. It's gone four in the morning. Helen's made no promises to me. We've not discussed the future. Maybe it would be best if I go. Only, when I try to leave the bed, her arm reaches over and squeezes my shoulder, as if asking me to stay.

'Are you all right?' she murmurs.

'I'm fine, but I can't sleep.'

'Talk to me then,' she says, though her eyes aren't open.

I know what I want to say, but I can't. Helen wouldn't leave Paul for me. Looking at her, I'm not even sure that I'd want her to. I have no idea where I'm going next. The magazine's over and I've lost interest in returning to university. I've still got most of the money Helen gave me. Maybe it's time to travel. I'm not ready to write yet, so what I need to do is have experiences, gather material.

'Why did you try to buy that book, earlier?' I ask her.

'What book?' She's not really awake.

'*User*.'

'Paul rang earlier. He wanted me to find him a copy.'

Her husband's name sends a chill through me. 'Did he say why?' I ask, but she's gone back to sleep. I wash and dress. Helen doesn't stir again. I kiss the nape of her neck, then let myself out of the room.

Downstairs, the doorman does not wish me 'goodnight' as I leave. Maybe he thinks I'm a gigolo who's been servicing a wealthy guest. This thought amuses me and I get an idea for a story that I'll start to write as soon as I get home.

Only that isn't possible for, as I walk through Leicester Square at five in the morning, I'm conscious of commotion, sirens, large vehicles trying to move through narrow alleys. There's a fire engine jammed between the Chinese supermarket and the triple X video store. I see a ladder rammed up the outer wall of the office. A policeman tells me to get back and I tell him that I live there, on the top floor. His attitude changes.

'Anybody else likely to be inside?'

'Not at night, no.'

'You're very lucky,' he tells me. 'If you'd been asleep upstairs when this lot started, you'd be a goner by now.'

This news has no effect on me, for I am already certain

about who was responsible for this fire, someone who knew I would not be home.

'Insured, are you?'

I shake my head. While I have lost a few paltry possessions, Tony has lost his nest egg, his legacy. He will be devastated.

'Pity,' the officer says, before going off to tell the firefighters that nobody's burning to death inside. I stare in horror when, on the top floor, there's a sudden conflagration. Flames shoot into the clear, cloudless, Soho sky. A small part of the history of English Literature is consumed, translated into smoke, never to be seen again.

Thirty-nine

Tony arrived a few minutes after me, frantic with worry that I was trapped inside. I called Helen at the hotel. Reception refused to put me through, saying they had instructions not to disturb her. By the time Tony and I made it back to his Highgate flat, early in the afternoon, there was a message from Paul on the answering machine.

'Heard what happened. That's really tough. Can't talk. Got a flight to catch. Ciao.'

'I'm a fool,' Tony said. 'If only I'd kept the stuff here. But it's only paper, in the end. You've lost everything.'

'At least I wasn't hurt,' I told him, adding, 'and I've still got most of the thousand Paul gave me in the bank.'

'I'll help as much as I can,' Tony told me. 'Stay here as long as you want.'

I thanked him. Tony was my partner in crime, my surrogate father, but I still had no desire to live with him.

'I think I'll go back to Leam for a while,' I said.

The next day found me there. I hadn't written ahead to say I was coming. Tim and Magneta had said I was welcome any time. I hoped they really meant it.

Spring arrived later in Leam than London. There were still bluebells in the small flower bed at the front of the cottage. Its front door was newly painted in a rich green. Magneta answered my knock. Her hair was longer and wilder and she had put on weight. She shrieked with delight and hugged me.

'We were only talking about you this morning,' she said, ushering me inside. 'We read about it in the papers.'

'You read about it?' I didn't realise that the fire had been reported.

'Yes. You were a big fan of his, weren't you?'

'Yes. I was. Am.' Now I thought she meant Sherwin.

'And so soon after him giving the story to the magazine.'

'How did you know about that?' I still thought she meant Sherwin. Magneta looked perplexed.

'I know because Tim was in the same issue. Mark, you do know what I'm talking about? It's just been on the radio. Graham Greene's dead. He died in Switzerland, yesterday. Mark, are you all right?'

My face must have gone pale. Greene had been ill for ages. He'd died, more or less, of old age. Even so, at that moment, I felt that I'd murdered him.

Forty

'Is this all the stuff you've brought?'

'It is.' My belongings fitted, with room to spare, into an old flight bag of Tony's. I was travelling light. 'Something happened.'

I told Magneta about the fire, how it had destroyed my flat, the archive, even the typewriter that Graham Greene had once written on.

'Was any of it insured?'

'I never bothered with insurance. Tony told me when I moved in that contents insurance cost too much. It was one reason he wanted me there.'

'What about your computer?'

'Gone.'

'With all your writing?'

'That was on discs, but they were in the fire, too.'

'Oh, Mark. All your work!'

'It doesn't matter.' I found myself telling the story of Hemingway in Paris, how Hadley lost all of his stories on the train, so he had to rewrite them.

'And in the end, you see, it worked out fine, because the rewritten stories were probably better than the originals.'

Only probably,' Magneta said. 'You can rewrite too much. Now we'll never know. Anyway, as I recall, Hemingway didn't rewrite everything he lost, not by a long shot. Didn't a couple of those stories turn up?'

'In Paris, yes.'

'I remember. Found by this shady literary dealer who married his foster daughter...'

'Step daughter. Funnily enough, I know them.' Hesitantly, because there was so much I had to leave out, I told Magneta how Paul Mercer had been on the verge of buying the *LR's* archives when the office burnt down.

'Don't you find that suspicious?' Magneta asked when I'd finished.

I found it suspicious. There was nothing about Paul Mercer that wasn't suspicious. But I couldn't tell Magneta how I knew that, nor where I was on the night of the fire. It was too embarrassing.

'I suggested the same to Tony, but he told me I was being paranoid. "What motive would Paul have for burning down the building?" he said.'

'He could have taken the archive first.'

'But he wouldn't be able to sell it. He'd be caught first time he tried. Paul wouldn't risk his reputation. No, I think we have to put it down to coincidence. The police reckon the fire started in the porn shop on the ground floor.'

I wasn't sure I believed this, but Magneta seemed to accept it.

'You're lucky you woke up,' she said. 'Were you in danger?'

'I wasn't there,' I admitted.

'You weren't... oh, Mark Trace, have you finally got a girl-friend?'

I shook my head, 'Only sort of.'

'Meaning?'

'Meaning she's married and her husband was out of town.'

'Mark!' Magneta gave me a look I hadn't seen before, one that mixed admiration with disdain.

I was still avoiding questions about this girlfriend when Tim came in. He was wearing a pale blue uniform. Seeing me, he whooped enthusiastically.

'You look well,' he told me.

'He's got a girlfriend,' Magneta whispered, sotto voce.

'It shows. Did you hear about Greene?'

'I heard. What's with the postman's uniform?'

'I've just finished work. I'm still writing. Don't worry. But with the baby on the way, we couldn't get by on what Magneta makes from her dirty books.'

'Baby?'

'She hasn't told you?'

'I thought he'd notice,' Magneta interjected, 'but he's only been here a few minutes.'

It was too much to take in: destruction, death, birth, going on all around me. I congratulated them from the bottom of my forger's heart.

That evening, we talked about what I would do next. I wanted to remain in London. I could always stay with Tony for a while. I should study for my first year retakes, then, in the autumn, begin my second year at university. Maybe I would switch courses. Maybe not. Money might be a problem, unless I managed to find work on another magazine.

'We should pay you more rent,' Magneta suggested.

'You're looking after the house, improving it. That's all I want.'

The day before I returned to London, the final issue of the *Little Review* arrived in the post. Tim and Magneta pored over it.

'He could still pull it off,' Tim said, gratifyingly, after reading my Sherwin story. 'I hope there's more where this came from.'

'So do I,' I said, though I would be worried if there was. The appearance of an extensive section of *A Commune* might demonstrate — especially if Sherwin had changed his style — that my version was a fake.

That night, Tim bought a bottle of scotch and we got drunk. Tim and I talked about our literary ambitions, about novels we wanted to write and the scene we wanted to be part of. Drink gave us confidence — our time would come. Maybe not until the next century. We were young, we could accept that. Possibly the novels we wanted to write were old fashioned, but then the form was an old one. We'd find ways to freshen it up, make our claim. Life, we agreed, was an inexhaustible subject.

As Tim got excited, he put CDs on: loud, punky music. He and Magneta danced. Fifteen minutes later, Tim flaked out. It was after ten and he'd been up since five. Magneta and I had to help him upstairs to bed. When that was done, I thought she'd join him, but neither of us was tired. So we went downstairs and talked, continuing the conversation in a more measured, cautious register.

'You haven't said much about your writing,' I ventured.

'The bottom's fallen out of the women's erotic novel,' Magneta told me. 'I'm not getting any new commissions.'

'I don't mean that,' I said. 'What about your real writing? It's ages since you sent anything to the *LR*. I know Tony asked you to contribute something for the final issue...'

Magneta sighed. 'All that's gone,' she said. 'I was never a real writer. I've got a bit of talent and I can give people what they want, whether it's a wank fantasy or a surreal, confessional monologue that makes editors like Tony think there's something there worth encouraging. But it's all fake. Tim's a real writer, working on his stuff every spare moment he can find, not bothered about who's going to buy it. I'm just a hack. I see a market and sell to it. When I try and write for myself, there's nothing there.'

I didn't know how to reply. 'You don't really mean that,' was all I said.

'I've been doing this for ten years. If I was on to something, I'd know by now.'

Forty-one

James Sherwin's memorial service was well attended. I recognised many of the people there. There were faces I'd either seen at literary events or recognised from dust jackets and newspapers. Amongst them were several young writers who couldn't possibly have known Sherwin, and whom you wouldn't have guessed could have been influenced by him. Maybe they weren't and, to them, the memorial service was just another literary beano, where it was important to see and be seen, before retiring to the Coach and Horses to network and catch up on gossip. Richard Mayfield walked straight past me without so much as a nod. Maybe he was lost in thought or perhaps he had been so drunk the evening we spent together that he'd forgotten my face. I preferred these scenarios to the more cynical one, that he was seeking out more influential people than me to sit next to.

It was the first service of this kind that I'd been to. As people arrived, there was taped music by (according to the order of service) the Grateful Dead and the Pink Floyd. Tony said a few words about Sherwin. A well known actor read the passage about death from *Stargazer*. This was followed by an excruciating attempt to get everyone to sing Bob Dylan's 'Blowing In The Wind'.

'The publisher's suggestion,' Tony whispered to me.

An organ played Bach, restoring calm, and we all filed out.

It was then I noticed him. Paul Mercer, not accompanied by his wife, walked rapidly out of the building. He ignored me and gave Tony only a brusque nod of the head. Paul was making a beeline for the chief mourner, Sonia Sherwin. We watched as he offered his sympathies.

'I'll bet the shit's after Jim's manuscripts,' Tony whispered.

There'd been some doubt as to whether Sonia could cope with leaving Greece to attend this service. Tony, who'd organised the event, hadn't known that Sonia was coming until she showed up in the front row of the church. I watched her now, pleased to see her give Paul short shrift, although she accepted the business card he proffered.

'I suppose I ought to introduce myself,' Tony said, when Paul left her. 'Would you like to meet the widow Sherwin?'

There was an informal queue of people wanting to offer their sympathies. We waited for it to clear.

Sonia Sherwin's body language was twitchy. She gave the impression she would prefer to be anywhere but where she was. Just as she thought she was clear of well wishers, Tony approached her. The widow flinched at having to talk to somebody else. When Tony introduced himself, she relaxed, but only a little.

'Thank you so much for organising this. I wouldn't have known where to begin. And thank you for sending Jim's manuscript. It was very interesting.'

Tony murmured a few words of sympathy, then introduced me.

'Mark Trace, my editorial assistant. He's a great admirer of your husband's writing.'

Mrs Sherwin held out a black gloved hand and I shook it.

'I'd appreciate it if we could meet before I return to Greece, Mr Bracken. Would you have the time?'

'Of course.'

I could see I wasn't wanted, so melted into the background. Paul Mercer was still nearby, his red face standing out all the more because of his black suit and tie. Impulsively, I decided to speak to him. I might glean whether he was behind the fire. Also, Tony had made inquiries on my behalf: the Hemingway manuscripts had been sold for a large sum, if not quite what was reported in the newspapers. I ought to tap Paul up for more money. And I wanted to know if he knew I'd slept with his wife.

Seeing me approach, Mercer dragged himself away from the elderly poet he'd been chatting up.

'Do we have something to discuss, Mark?' Mercer's tone was mildly aggressive.

'You know we do,' I said, then added, provoking him. 'How's Helen?'

'She's busy furnishing the townhouse we've just bought in the Village.'

'You must give me your new address,' I said to him.

Paul eyed me coldly. 'What do you want, Mark?'

'Tony tells me that you sold the Hemingway stories, several months ago.'

'Yes, that's true.'

'You lied to me.'

'You lied to me about finding them,' Paul pointed out. 'Selling those fake manuscripts could have ruined my reputation.'

'Instead, it made you.'

'In a way,' Paul admitted. 'But not in the way I would have chosen. All that publicity was very embarrassing for Helen.'

'We never agreed what your percentage was,' I told him, businesslike.

'No, we didn't,' Paul said. 'As far as I'm concerned, I found those stories. There are plenty of people who'll remember Helen and me trawling through the flea-market, looking in old copies of *Paris Match*. Our story stands up. Whereas your story — what is it, exactly? That you found the stories, as you told Helen? No proof. That you faked the stories and I took them from you? Again, no proof. And even if you were able to prove that you forged those stories, you couldn't establish that I knew about them, because I didn't. My reputation as a dealer would hardly suffer. Your reputation as — whatever you think you are — would be ruined.'

'But I could prove that you didn't pay me for the stories,' I argued.

'Oh but I did,' Paul said. 'You accepted a thousand pounds. I didn't ask for a receipt, so you may have avoided paying tax on it, but I have a very good witness who'll tell any court that you not only took the money, but you also accepted various goods in kind that were paid for from my credit card account. You did well out of me, Mark. Now, let it drop.'

My face burned. But I wouldn't leave it.

'What do you know about the fire?' I asked, and as soon as these crass words were out of my mouth, I regretted them.

'I know you were lucky,' Paul told me. 'Lucky that all evidence of your forgeries went up in smoke, lucky that Graham Greene died when he did, lucky you weren't in the building when it happened. Where were you, Mark?'

I didn't answer this, but I didn't have to. Paul Mercer was the sort of man who only asked questions to which he already knew the answer. He knew I'd fucked his wife and he didn't care. Maybe he had even persuaded Helen to seduce me, but I couldn't countenance that, not then.

'If you stay in this game,' Paul lectured me, 'our paths will probably cross again. So remember this. You can't beat me. Whereas I know enough to destroy you.' He gave me a broad smile and turned round. 'Hey, Tony! Good to see you. Nice service, but I've got to run. I really liked that last issue you did. You went out in style, gotta give you that.'

We watched him scuttle away.

'What did the widow want?' I asked Tony.

'I don't know. I'm meeting her again later in the week, after she's seen both sets of Jim's publishers.'

'You don't think she suspects?'

'Suspicion doesn't come into it. She either knows, or she doesn't know.'

Next day, I went to the British Library, where I found a facsimile edition of the recently discovered Paris Hemingway stories. My original few pages had been expanded into an expensive hardback, newly published by a university press. It had a scholarly introduction, extensive footnotes and my variant text for *Out Of Season*. Skimming the pages, I found it hard to believe I'd been so obsessed with the macho Hemingway, when I could have spent my time in Paris retracing the steps of Beckett or Joyce. Saul Bellow, I'd since discovered, had written most of his best novel there. I was over Hemingway, but my fakes were part of the canon. The reviews I'd seen had been respectful, convinced that Paul Mercer had made an important find. His reputation as a manuscript dealer rested on these two stories. Nothing would give me greater delight than to fuck him up.

I held one trump card Paul Mercer didn't know about. But I couldn't decide how to play my hand. I didn't want to claim credit for my forgeries. I wanted to discredit Paul Mercer as a dealer in valuable manuscripts.

That evening, I tried to explain all this to Tony, who was in unusually good spirits. As we talked, I hit upon the answer.

'I know exactly what to do,' I told my friend.

'And are you going to tell me?' Tony asked.

'I won't involve you. But I'll need to go to France, in a week or so. I lost my bank card in the fire and I'm waiting for a new one. Can you lend me some cash for a plane ticket?'

'No problem,' Tony said. 'The bank has increased my overdraft limit now I have an insurance payout on the way.'

'I thought the offices weren't insured?'

'The buildings were insured, but by the owners. I only had a lease. The office contents were never insured. However, after agreeing a price with Mercer, I insured the archive. Once I knew what it was worth I'd've been mad not to.'

'Astute,' I said.

Tony could be flaky in his personal life, but never where the magazine was concerned.

'How much do you need?'

He offered me a generous amount. It would take me a few days to get a new passport. That was OK, because there was something I needed to do first.

Forty-two

'Are you going to explain why you need the typewriter all of a sudden?'

Out of breath, I didn't reply. I'd written to Francine and she'd collected the machine from the friend's house where it was stashed. I'd met her taxi and was carrying the machine up to my hotel room in the seventh arrondissement.

At sixteen Francine was the beauty I'd anticipated when she was fourteen. She had lost all of her gawkiness. Once I'd put the machine down, I wanted nothing more than to take up where her father had interrupted us in the summer of '89. But she wanted to talk about the typewriter.

'You're going to do another forgery, aren't you? Do you still have any of the right paper?'

'It doesn't matter,' I told her.

'You must tell me everything. We never had secrets before.'

Her English had become more sophisticated than my French, so we spoke in my language. When I was done, she clapped her hands.

'I think it will work, if I help you. But I don't understand why you're so determined to expose your own forgeries.'

Hesitantly, I told her the rest of it, up to and including the point where the office burnt down while I slept with Helen. Francine was not in the least shocked.

'You think they planned it all, that her husband stole the documents?'

'Not all the documents,' I said. 'Maybe a few of the most valuable ones — things that he can sell to collectors who won't mind their not being able to show them in public. Or he'll save them for a few years, then sell after Tony's dead.'

'He whored his own wife for papers worth a few thousand

pounds! Didn't you say he was a rich man?'

'"Rich people stay that way by holding onto their money",
Tony says. Anyhow, I don't know if Helen was in on it. We'd
become very close. She knew how I felt about her. I think she
was starting to feel that way about me. Maybe Paul used her,
the way he used...'

Even as I said this, I knew how pathetic it sounded. I
remembered Helen was keen we went to her hotel room, not
the office, on the night of my birthday.

'You poor romantic,' Francine said, stroking my hair.

'I'm over her now,' I assured her.

She kissed me on the cheek. Then she told me she had to
go. We arranged to meet again the following day.

When Francine was gone, I got out some paper. The sheets
looked the same as the sheets I'd typed my first Hemingway
stories on. They had a similar, brittle feel, but were of English
manufacture, and only twenty years old.

I'd determined to give up forgery after the Sherwin story.
Yet it seemed that, whenever I stopped, a burning necessity
arose, sucking me back in. I had already drafted what I was
going to type. The forgery had to be as good as the others, if
not better. But I needn't feel any guilt, or fear. This time, I was
planning to get caught.

Forty-three

The address on the receipt was easy to find. The old lady was still alive, and at home. She invited us up to her cramped apartment. Francine did the bulk of the talking, giggling as if playing the part of a favourite granddaughter, disarming Madame Devonier. Without her, I suspect, the discussion that followed would have been much less *complaisant*.

Madame Devonier was eighty-three but her mind was still sharp. She'd heard of the Hemingway stories, seen the *Paris Match* article. It amused her to know that the stories were forgeries, typed on the machine she had sold to me. But she couldn't understand why I wanted to give the machine back. Francine said my behaviour was an example of the peculiar British sense of humour. Then she explained. Madame laughed a lot and opened the bottle of wine we'd brought with us. Once it became clear that she stood to make some money out of our plan, she became positively enthusiastic. As we drank the wine, Madame Devonier rehearsed the story she would tell, asking questions now and then. Relaxing into her role, she began adding details of her own that would increase the tale's authenticity. Francine and I played the part of journalists, taking it in turns to quiz her.

Later that afternoon, a little drunk and still excited by our visit to Madame Devonier, Francine and I returned to my hotel room, for reasons we hadn't discussed. There was no foreplay or seduction, not unless you count my taking Francine's hand as we climbed the stairs. We were doing the inevitable. She was more experienced than me, but not very much so. I was grateful, as we undressed, that I had already been with Helen and had some idea of what to do. But there was no need to worry. Francine and I were easy with each other: passionate and friendly. Neither of us behaved as though our lives depended on this one act.

Afterwards, I would have promised to move back to Paris there and then, had Francine agreed to be my girlfriend. Only she already had a boyfriend, of whom she didn't speak, and had to return home for dinner at seven to parents who wouldn't abide me. Next day, she had to go to school. I had to go back to England. I had no more chance of a future with her than I had with Helen.

That evening, when I returned with the typewriter, I worried that Madame Devonier might have changed her mind. But she hadn't. I heaved the typewriter into her spare room, cleaned it carefully to avoid fingerprints, then watched as the old lady covered it in dust, swept from the top of an old wardrobe.

Forty-four

The meeting with Sonia Sherwin was to take place in her hotel suite the day after my return from France. In the taxi, on our way there, Tony gave me a belated warning about the Hemingway plan.

'Paul Mercer did well out of your Hemingway forgeries. But you weren't going to sell them. You haven't lost anything... yet. By exposing that the stories were faked, you may expose yourself. You want to be a writer, but you're risking your reputation before you start.'

'Mercer can't bring me into it without revealing how he really got the stories.'

'He's cleverer than you give him credit for. A man like Mercer is good at revenge. He might sit on your secret for years, then decide to expose you just when you're making a name for yourself.'

'It's a risk I'm willing to take.'

Sonia Sherwin was an elegant American woman with dark, Italianate features. She was forty but looked five years younger. Sonia wore black, confidently allowing the odd fleck of grey to highlight her dark hair. With her aristocratic air, the widow could have been a smaller, older version of Helen Mercer. She talked about James Sherwin as though she were describing a historical figure, rather than a husband.

'When I first met him, he'd stopped writing altogether. That novel you published part of, he'd abandoned it years ago.'

Her words were addressed to Tony. I sat to his side, trying to work out whether she'd sussed us. So far, we seemed to be in the clear.

'Pity,' Tony said.

'As I told you in my letter, I am Jim's literary executor. He left very strict instructions on what was to be preserved. There are barely enough good unpublished or uncollected pieces to fill a slim book. Jim didn't want to rehash anything that would harm his reputation.'

'I'm sure that wouldn't happen,' Tony murmured.

'My husband used to speak about the terrible Hemingway stuff that got published decades after he died. Jim wasn't satisfied by most of his output, even when he was at his peak. He destroyed nearly everything he wrote in the last twenty years.'

'Nearly *everything*?' Tony said, sounding alarmed. I wondered if the Hemingway comment was a sly dig. Probably not. The poor quality of Hemingway's late work was one reason why the recent discovery of early material from his nascent, vital years had been greeted with such excitement.

'His publishers have been on to me, Tony. They'd given up on *A Commune* years ago. The contract was cancelled. But they love what you published. They say if they put something out quickly it will sell in vast quantities. They think Jim must have been getting ready to finish the thing. They don't understand why I'm reluctant to hand everything over. But I expect you do.'

She held up a copy of the final edition of the *Little Review*. This issue had had the largest print run of the magazine's history, staying on shop shelves for less than two weeks before it completely sold out. Sonia's voice became cold, toneless.

'I was surprised when this contained an extract from *A Commune*, especially as I'd watched Jim burn his only copy of the unfinished, handwritten manuscript. It was a huge weight off his mind, he told me at the time.'

'Jim was always a perfectionist,' Tony murmured. 'But...'

He thought better of finishing the sentence. Sonia was reaching into a cheap, brown cardboard box at the side of her chair.

'You were good enough to send me the original print-out of the extract Jim sent you.' She took some loose leaf pages out of the box, held them up. 'Mark, would you like a look at the stuff Jim was working on when he died?'

'Very much,' I said.

'They're more memoir than fiction, and very fragmentary, not publishable as they stand. I printed them off before I left the island. I wanted a hard copy in case there was anything wrong with the disks. But I haven't had time to separate the pages.'

She rested the loose leaf sheets on the carpet, then began to pull a stack of cheap, thin computer paper out of the box. To make such paper A4 in size, you needed to tear narrow strips from each side, every strip punctured where the sheets were held by the roller. Then you must tear the perforated pages apart. Sonia concertinaed the connected sheets in front of us.

'This was the only kind of paper Jim used for his creative work,' she told me. 'With single sheets, you have to stand by the printer and feed it in a page at a time. Jim didn't have the patience for that.'

'Maybe...' Tony began, but Sonia silenced him with a glare. She picked up the final issue of the *Little Review* again, opening it at the Sherwin story.

'Jim didn't write this. I want to know who did.'

Forty-five

As Sonia Sherwin was interrogating us, an interrogation of a different kind was taking place across the English channel. Madame Devonier was busy telling journalists about her amazing find. She had rung *Paris Match* first. Several papers had beat a path to the old lady's door and listened to her well rehearsed story. Madame Devonier insisted that, for months, she hadn't realised the famous 'Hemingway' stories came from her flat. One day a friend suggested the stories might have been discovered in the old copies of *Paris Match* she had taken to the flea market two years earlier. Madame Devonier went through the rest of the magazines she kept under the bed in her spare room.

After her discovery, she didn't at first consider the old typewriter, which still sat above the wardrobe in the same room. She was too excited by having found the third story, which turned out to be a previously unknown piece, one Hemingway never rewrote. She hoped it would make her rich. But the typeface on the story was worryingly familiar. She occasionally typed letters on the old machine. The last time that the typewriter was used by another person, she realised, would have been twenty years ago, just after she was widowed. That summer, a young American had rented her spare room for a couple of months.

No, after all this time, she couldn't remember the young man's name, but he had borrowed the typewriter, with her permission. It was never used often. She recalled there was some very old paper with it. The lodger finished this paper off and replaced it. He left in a hurry, owing two weeks rent, she remembered that. The old *Paris Match* magazines were kept in the spare room for visitors to read. He must have stashed his stories amongst them before he left.

Were the Hemingway stories a deliberate attempt to defraud the finder? Not on her behalf. Maybe on the young American's. After so many years, who could guess his intentions? It could be that the stories were an exercise he practised to pass the time while he was supposed to be studying French. She recalled that his spoken French was not very good.

Madame Devonier was too honest a person to profit from a forgery. She didn't know whether this last story would be worth anything. But even forgeries had a monetary value, she had read somewhere, if they became famous enough. So she had gone to the journalists, seeking advice.

In the weeks that followed, the university that had bought the Hemingway manuscripts allowed comparison tests to be done. There was no doubt: the 'new' Hemingway story was typed on the same typewriter as the other pieces, a Royal, the same brand of machine Hemingway used in the twenties. However, while the first two stories had been typed on paper at least seventy years old, this third one was on paper a good fifty years younger.

As soon as the forgery was proved, other, previously suppressed, doubts began to circulate. Some of the typical Hemingway 'mistakes' in each story seemed a little studied. Literary critics remarked that the writing in the 'previously unknown' piece verged on parody.

Madame Devonier got a good price for a faked manuscript. *Different Ways Of Getting Drunk* was published in *The New York Review Of Books*. Anybody who wanted could do their own comparisons. In due course, at least three men came forward as the 'author of the great Hemingway hoax'. All claimed to have spent the summer of 1971 in Paris. Madame Devonier refuted each one.

Paul Mercer had no choice but to throw himself at the mercy of the Texas university. He had been completely taken in, he said. In his defence, all he could offer was that he had found the stories in the way he described, then had them authenticated by experts whose opinion he had no reason to doubt. Nobody questioned this account. Nevertheless, Mercer's reputation took a big knock. If, as I suspected, he had stolen the cream of the *Little Review* archive before setting fire to the office, he would have even more trouble selling it. From then on, nobody was going to buy a manuscript from him unless its provenance was perfect.

Forty-six

When Tony finished talking, I was too ashamed to speak.

'Well?'

I tried to say 'I'm sorry', but Sonia gave me a stare of such ferocity, I wished I could shrink and hide inside my clothes. Tony and I didn't as much as glance at each other. Heads bowed, we waited for her verdict.

Tony's explanation had been craven, pleading the magazine's imminent demise as an excuse, if not a justification. I couldn't tell how much sense this made to Sonia. It made little to me. The Sherwin story had helped sales. Yet, while the last issue had sold out, it was always likely to sell out. Tony couldn't afford to print extra copies, or order a reprint. Until the insurance money came through, he was broke. Neither of us had profited from my Sherwin forgery. We hadn't done this one for money. We'd forged for the thrill of it. Because we could.

'You said the magazine published another of Mark's faked stories,' Sonia said. 'Was the writer of that one dead, too?'

'No.' Tony told her about the Graham Greene story. 'But Graham guessed someone was pulling my leg. It amused him, I think.'

'Do you think James would have been amused? Is that your defence?'

'There's no defence,' I said. 'We were in the wrong. I'm sorry.'

She ignored me.

'How do you think it will look?' she asked Tony, 'when you own up? You're a respected poet, James admired your work. You should be receiving honours, appearing at literary festivals, winning prizes. Instead, you'll be notorious for betraying a friend. The invitations won't come. You'll be a pariah.'

Tony's face was pallid. The gravity of his situation was starting to sink in. She turned to me.

'You must have some respect for literature, to be working for a magazine like Tony's when you're so young. And you must be talented, to convince so many people. You're not original, but maybe that would have come, with maturity. What did you plan to do with your life?'

'I wanted to write,' I admitted. 'Novels.' Then I added, truthfully, 'your husband was my hero.'

'Didn't you realise? Once this gets out, any literary career you might have had will be over before it's begun.'

'There must be a way I can make amends,' I pleaded. I thought of telling her about the Hemingway stories and how I was planning to expose them. But I'd be digging myself into an even deeper hole. Best not to mention Dahl either.

'I've been trying to decide what Jim would have wanted,' Sonia said. 'He liked you, Tony. He respected you. If he'd written anything he thought was worthy of your magazine, he'd have sent it to you. He was reckless about money. It wouldn't have bothered him that he could have made a small fortune publishing it elsewhere. But it would have disturbed him to see you utterly humiliated, destroyed.'

'I'll do anything...' Tony began.

'Yes,' Sonia interrupted, 'you will. But, for the moment, you'll keep quiet. I don't want a word of this to leak out.'

'You must forgive Mark,' he said. 'He's very young and he was only trying to help.'

'Not too young to go to prison,' she said. 'Leave him with me. You can go home now.'

'But, what...?'

'You'll find out in due course.'

As he left the room, with his back to Sonia, Tony gave one

of his hopeless shrugs. He flashed a sympathetic smile in my direction. There was still a little mischief in it. He thought we were getting off lightly.

When we were alone, Sonia at last turned to me. I tried to meet her long, hard gaze, but couldn't. She was so frostily beautiful, so scary, and I was so guilty. My eyes drifted to the small coffee table beside her. The computer disks containing her husband's last few pages lay on it, underlining my outrageous behaviour. I could hardly begin to imagine the mind of a writer who would only allow his very best work to be published. I would never have that kind of integrity, or dignity.

'What do you want me to do?' I asked.

She told me.

Forty-seven

Three weeks after my meeting with Sonia Sherwin, I was back in the small living room of my house in Leam. Magneta, tired by her pregnancy, had gone to bed. Tim and I were finishing off a second bottle of wine.

'We'll miss you,' Tim said, 'but it does sound exciting.'

'It's too good an opportunity to turn down,' I said, trying to sound enthusiastic. 'But I hope I can make it back in time for the christening.'

Living with Tony had become uncomfortable. He was the only person I was allowed to tell about my 'punishment'. But neither of us wanted to talk about it. At first, I'd kept my head down and revised for my first year retakes. While I waited for the results I realised that, with the magazine gone, we had less and less in common. So I came to Leam.

Tim and I discussed the Hemingway forgeries, news of which had been all over the broadsheets. I couldn't tell Tim that I was responsible for them. If I revealed that much, he would work out the rest.

'I remember you telling me about Mercer,' Tim said. 'He was the guy who was going to buy the *Little Review* archive before the fire.'

'The one whose wife I was sleeping with on the night of the fire.'

'Jeez. You never told us who she was before.'

I was drunk, or I wouldn't have let my guard slip. I badly wanted to tell Tim how I really got to know Helen, how I'd wanted her and obsessed over her long before I knew she was Mercer's mistress. But once I started it would be difficult to know where to stop.

'Come on,' Tim said. 'Spill the beans.'

Since Magneta wasn't there, I could describe my seduction without becoming embarrassed. Even so, I kept the account brief, emphasising Helen's 'open marriage', trying to come over more used than user. Whatever words I used, it still sounded like a tacky episode.

'When I saw Mercer at Sherwin's funeral, he *knew*. But I find it hard to believe he set the situation up. I think the fire was a coincidence.'

'I don't believe in coincidences,' Tim said.

'We'll only know for certain if those manuscripts appear on the market,' I told him. 'I'll bet they don't. Mercer's survived two scandals. Even if he did steal some of the archive, I can't see him risking a third.'

'Don't be so sure,' Tim told me. 'Some people are addicted to risk.'

I returned to Highgate to collect my stuff and say goodbye. I still had some of the cash Tony had loaned me for the Paris escapade, but Tony insisted on giving me a large sum in traveller's cheques as well.

'You don't want to be completely reliant on Sonia Sherwin.'

'I don't have much choice. She's got me by the balls.'

'Both of us,' Tony said, then rose, creakily, from his armchair. 'I want to show you a couple of things.'

He handed me a letter from Roald Dahl's agent. This venerable gent stated that he could find no trace of Dahl ever having written a story called *The Woman Who Married Herself*. 'It's pretty good but there's something not right about it,' the agent wrote. 'The main problem is that there is no record of Dahl having sent a story of this title to his typist. Dahl himself never learned to type and this has rather too many errors for it to be the work of a professional typist.'

'You reckoned without that information,' Tony said.

The idea of a modern author who couldn't type staggered me. I managed a hollow laugh. To think that I had gone to all that trouble to borrow a typewriter which its owner never learned how to use. Tony gave one of his wry smiles and changed the subject.

'How long do you think it'll take you to do?' he asked.

'It'll take as long as it takes. Tim and Magneta want me to be godfather to their baby, but I don't suppose I'll have finished by the time it's born. I don't even know if Sonia Sherwin will let me come back for the christening. At least the university don't seem bothered about my taking another year out.'

'I wish I could be there to help you.'

'I'll write to you, if she lets me.'

Tony nodded, a distracted look in his eyes. I stood.

'I'd better get to the airport.'

'I'll pay for a taxi,' Tony said, lifting himself once more from the armchair, supporting himself with the cane that he had begun to use all the time. He phoned for a cab. 'Before you go, there's something I have to show you. You may hate me for this, but I'll hate myself more if I let you go without telling you what really happened.'

I followed him down to the basement. There, he showed me a multitude of manuscripts and envelopes. They were in cardboard boxes and plastic bags rather than the old tea chests I had methodically sorted through. Nevertheless, I knew exactly what they were.

'You? You stole the archive, not Phil Mercer!'

'Can you forgive me for deceiving you?'

Back upstairs, in his dusty flat, Tony confessed that he had painstakingly planned and executed the Soho fire himself, tracking my pursuit of Helen until he was sure I would be out all night. At his signal, an acquaintance of the equally well insured porn store owner set alight the shop below the office. Both beneficiaries had unimpeachable alibis.

'I knew Paul Mercer would find a way to rip me off over the archive, but the insurance company wouldn't.'

Tony had taken home most of the best stuff and planned to sell it privately, piecemeal, over the next few years. He'd worked out how to make his retirement plan pay up twice. Devious old sod.

'Without Mercer's offer, I couldn't have insured the archive for anything like as much. He did me a favour, in a sense.'

'I wish you'd found a way to take his money off him, too.'

'Don't harbour grudges,' Tony advised me. 'You got your revenge by exposing the fake Hemingways. Mercer's no worse a shark than plenty of others out there.'

The taxi sounded its horn.

'Write to me if you can,' Tony begged. 'I'll be lonely.'

'You'll enjoy retirement,' I said. 'Time to catch up with loads of people.'

'Editors who have ceased to edit soon lose most of their friends,' he told me. 'But we'll stay friends, won't we? Despite it all.'

'Despite it all,' I repeated, and hugged him goodbye.

Forty-eight

Ghosts aren't real, rational people know that. They're in our heads. A trick of memory. I've never believed in ghosts. But now I am one.

In her Bloomsbury hotel, after Tony had left, Sonia told me that Sherwin's books have never sold as well as his reputation might suggest. His royalties have dwindled since the 70s. They barely provided enough for one person to get by on. Sonia spent all of her savings supporting Sherwin. Now she wants a larger inheritance.

Before I left London I wrote to Francine. I longed to tell her the truth. Instead I told her the same tale I'd given Tim and Magneta. Tony had been commissioned to write the authorised biography of James Sherwin. I was flying to Greece to collect material for him.

At Athens airport I caught a bus to the port of Piraeus. The bus had no air conditioning and the heat was stifling. Piraeus was worse. I spent hours sweltering, clinging to scraps of shade. There were no longer any direct ferries to Karenos. There was, however, one ferry a day that would take me to its nearest neighbour. After a long voyage I had to wait another day for the final leg of my journey. I was to catch the supply boat that, twice a week, took provisions to Karenos.

All of this waiting around gave me plenty of time to think about what I was doing. I used to believe that there was a profound infallibility about the way the world recognised great writing. But if Tony has taught me one thing about the literary world, it is this: luck and timing are far more important than talent. Once successful writers reach a certain status, people applaud anything they've touched, regardless of its quality.

None of my forgeries are wonderful pieces of writing. I got better as I went on, exercising whatever tiny muscle of talent I possess, but that was not the reason for my stories' success. They were believed because they appeared in the right place at the right time. They were believed because their readers wanted to believe.

Back in London, Sonia Sherwin told me how, because my Sherwin forgery had been so warmly received, she was being offered large sums of money for her husband's final novel. But the offers were conditional. Publishers wanted to see more before forking out. Sonia had nothing else to show them. There was much anticipation, the publishers told Sonia. The cheque was waiting. How long would it take her to edit her husband's papers? Sonia said that she would return to Karenos and consider the matter, only selling the manuscript when the time was right.

In the years before he burnt the manuscript, James Sherwin allowed his wife to read a few sections of *A Commune*. Her recollections, however, are garbled and unreliable. That's why she needs me to make the story up. In London, I warned Sonia that any book I wrote was likely to damage Sherwin's reputation. No matter, she said. Sonia, it turns out, is a practical woman. Her scruples are outweighed by need. And greed, some would say, but I am not in a position to criticise.

During the long wait for the Karenos supply boat, I began to doubt that I retained the ability to step inside another writer's style. I doubted whether any writer could pull off the vast forgery that Sonia requires of me. I used to believe there was something sacred about the creative process. I thought that real writers knew divine secrets. I hoped that, if I worked hard enough, these secrets would be revealed to me. I can't afford to think like that any more. I'm on the lookout for shortcuts.

When the boat arrived, I followed Sonia Sherwin's instructions. As soon as the old craft was secured to the harbour, I identified myself. Enormous seagulls squawked loudly overhead. There was no breeze. Despite the temperature, the boatman wore a black donkey jacket and a navy blue cap with a decorative pleat over the peak. His face was tanned and lined. I was motioned to wait nearby, in the full sun. I asked him about return times, thinking ahead to when my godchild is born, but did not get a clear reply. I have since discovered that George is a loyal friend of Sonia's. He will not take me off the island unless she tells him to. No matter. Should I find a means to escape, I have decided not to take it. I will keep my word and perform my penance.

It's easy to see why Sherwin made this place his home. There are no near neighbours. The days are long and peaceful. Most afternoons, a gentle breeze wafts through the pines, making the heat bearable. When I want a break, there is good swimming at the bottom of the hill. A man can lose himself here.

Sonia does not rush me. A complete novel, as she knows all too well, is tougher to write than an extract or a short story. Sonia answers my questions. She shows me around the island. She cooks simple meals. Mostly, she leaves me alone, with nothing to do but write.

James Sherwin was in his fifties when he died. I am only twenty, although, some days, I feel much older. I have Sherwin's library, and his collected works. But I don't have his wisdom or his talent. I don't have his experience. I sit in Sherwin's book lined study for hours on end. When I'm stuck for words, I play tricks on myself to make the inspiration flow. Sherwin's computer is identical to the one I lost in the fire. I imagine myself back in my Soho garret, forging my favourite writer for love, with no thought of publication. I try to summon up the innocence I once had.

A Commune was to be Sherwin's epic. But he was economical. Only one novel lasted more than fifty thousand words. I might get away with sixty. At the rate I'm going, that will take forever. I have a few thousand faked words to build on. These act as a touchstone for the rest. Every day I delete most of what I write, then edit away the previous day's work for good measure. When I can't get any further I turn to this memoir. I need to remind myself who I am, or used to be. Only his voice creeps into mine as mine creeps into his, until I can't tell which is which. Sherwin's ghost is always here, looking over my shoulder. He mocks me, the perpetual pretender, impersonating a man whose shoes he can never hope to fill.

Most days, though, I sit down at the damned machine, try.